Dear Readers,

Mother Nature may have turned up the heat, but nothing could be hotter than four sizzling new romances from Bouquet.

Get ready for two very different weddings! *Affaire de Coeur* raved about Suzanne Barrett's first Bouquet. This month she offers **Wild Irish Rogue,** a lively romp involving a green card, a favor of the matrimonial kind—and, of course, true love. In **The Bride's Best Man,** veteran Meteor author Laura Phillips gives us the story of a woman preparing to walk down the aisle—and wondering if her sexy childhood friend is really the man who should be at her side.

No one can pick out a bridal gown until she finds the right man—even if she finds him in the most unexpected place. A single dad is **Falling for Grace** in Maddie James's latest offering about neighbors who can get close in the sweetest way possible. Finally, a legacy of love and a decades-old jewel heist provide the backdrop for one clashing couple's **Stolen Kisses** from Kate Donovan.

Why not pack a Bouquet in your beach bag and let us show you just how good romance can be?

Kate Duffy
Editorial Director

"YOU'RE A CRIMINAL!"

After an instant of panic, she knew it was Locke, and knew further that she wasn't going to be able to pull off indignation over this manhandling—not with the official FBI documents strewn all over the bedroom floor.

"Let me explain—"

He began gathering the pages, methodically stuffing the folder. "Instead of profiling arsonists, we should be working on the Galloway Gang. Lying, manipulating and now stealing. Maybe I shouldn't have ruled your grandmother out as a suspect so quickly." He eyed the memo Josie had been reading. "Hand it over."

"Let me finish this one as least. I was only—" She grimaced as he began to tug it from her hand. "You're going to tear it, Locke. And you're going to wake Grandma."

He loosened his grip on the document. "One way or another, it's coming with me." Throwing Josie over his shoulder, memo and all, he headed toward the living room, where he dropped her on the sofa bed and pounced on her, imprisoning her limbs with his own. "Give me the memo."

"It's yours," she gasped, releasing the sheet of paper, which floated onto the floor. "Now get off me, you big jackass."

"Not so fast. I want to talk to you."

She flushed at the husky quality of his voice. They were too close, and it was too dark, and there definitely wasn't enough fabric protecting them from each other. Thin flannel and silky, cotton-candy–colored satin were simply not up to this particular erotic challenge.

"First of all, apologize for stealing my files."

"I was just borrowing them and you know it," Josie retorted.

"Fine. That's how you want to play it?" Without further warning, he lowered his mouth to her neck and began to explore it.

"Locke, this is a bad idea. Oh . . ." She sighed with reluctant pleasure as his lips began to caress her ear. For a bad idea, this was beginning to feel amazingly good . . .

STOLEN KISSES

KATE DONOVAN

Zebra Books
Kensington Publishing Corp.

http://www.zebrabooks.com

ZEBRA BOOKS are published by

Kensington Publishing Corp.
850 Third Avenue
New York, NY 10022

Copyright © 2000 by Kate Donovan

All rights reserved. No part of this book may be reproduced in any form or by any means without the prior written consent of the Publisher, excepting brief quotes used in reviews.

If you purchased this book without a cover you should be aware that this book is stolen property. It was reported as "unsold and destroyed" to the Publisher and neither the Author nor the Publisher has received any payment for this "stripped book."

Zebra and the Z logo Reg. U.S. Pat. & TM Off.

First Printing: July, 2000
10 9 8 7 6 5 4 3 2 1

Printed in the United States of America

ONE

All too aware of the smirks from patrolmen and detectives alike, Josie Galloway forced herself to remain calm and collected as she passed them on her way to the front desk of the Sutterville police station. These guys would love nothing better than to see her come unglued, and of course, she could hardly blame them. They were still smarting from her recent courtroom victory—a victory that had made them look like the Keystone Kops. Still, until today, she never would have believed them capable of using a sweet elderly lady as a means of avenging themselves.

"Josie! Wait up."

She spun to glare at Detective Pete Hanover. "Tell me that the message on my voice mail was a hoax, and you don't have my seventy-five-year-old grandma locked up in this hellhole."

Hanover's gray eyes twinkled. "I knew you'd go crazy, but don't blame *us* for all this. She's here, but it's the FBI that's talking to her."

"The FBI?"

"Right. And don't blame *them* either. Caroline's the one who insisted on coming 'downtown.' All the agent wanted to do was ask her a few routine questions at her house. No big deal."

"No big deal?" Josie eyed him suspiciously. "What kind of routine questioning? And who exactly is this agent?"

The detective shrugged. "A guy named Harper. He seems nice enough."

"Nice guys don't browbeat old ladies."

Hanover chuckled. "Believe me, Caroline's fine. She congratulated me on my engagement, showed me pictures of the great-grandkids, and even had us wheel a TV into the room so she could watch her soap opera. I think she's getting a big kick out of this—like she's Agatha Christie or something."

Josie smiled reluctantly. "What's going on, Pete? The message said Grandma was refusing to cooperate without her attorney present."

He nodded. "That's true enough. Apparently she witnessed some robbery, years ago. They reopened the case recently and wanted to ask her some follow-up questions. No biggie." With a mischievous smile he added, "The message shook you up? I thought you hotshot lawyers never lost your cool."

She grimaced but admitted, "I thought this might be your way of paying me back for the Parker fiasco."

"Give us a little credit, counselor. As much as me and the other guys would love to make you squirm for getting that car thief off the hook, we wouldn't use an old lady. Especially not Caroline."

"*Alleged* car thief," she corrected playfully. "Next time, remember to read him his rights. How hard can it be? You guys *can* read, can't you?"

Hanover's jaw tightened visibly. "You're too much, Josie. If you think we're so stupid, why do you keep hanging around us?"

"I've sworn off for good," she assured him. "Not just off cops but soldiers and cowboys and any other guy who carries a gun and thinks he's God's gift to women."

"Yeah?" The detective's face relaxed into a smirk. Have you sworn off guys with handcuffs, too?"

Josie smiled and patted his cheek. "I'd love to stay and trade insults, dear, but I need to take Grandma home. She's probably exhausted. Is the FBI guy around so I can get some details first?"

"He's in the interrogation room with her."

"He's *with* her? Without *me* there? After she distinctly requested—"

"Give him hell." Hanover grinned. "I already warned him that you're a pain in the ass. But just for the record, he's been treating her like a princess. I made sure of that."

"Thanks." She studied her former suitor fondly. "I guess I should congratulate you on your engagement too. It's pretty romantic, Detective Hanover. You catch the guy who's been stalking her and end up marrying her. It's like a fairy tale."

"Yeah, it's wild. But"—he flushed slightly—"it's great too."

Josie kissed his reddened face. "It couldn't happen to a nicer guy. I'm sorry I called you 'scum' during the trial."

"You called me 'the stuff scum scrapes off its shoes,' " he reminded her dolefully.

"Well, I take it all back. Now, I'd better go rescue Grandma from the FBI."

"Or vice versa." Hanover grinned again. "Want me to come along?"

"I can handle it." Summoning her most confident smile, Josie turned and hurried down the hall. When she reached the door to the interrogation room, she paused to take a deep, strengthening breath. First impressions were crucial, and she wanted the agent to see her as a formidable opponent not an emotional granddaughter. Sentiment aside, she was fully capable of nailing him to the wall, shield and all. The sooner he found that out, the better.

Still, Pete had said the situation was basically harmless, and so, when she pushed open the door, she allowed her smile to warm slightly.

Her gaze fell first on gray-haired, porcelain-skinned Caroline Galloway, sitting primly and properly in her best lavender suit, looking toward the doorway with obvious pride and anticipation. Josie might have beamed in return, but instead her expression froze as she spied the contents of her grandmother's purse strewn carelessly across the top of the interrogation table. "What the hell is *this?* Grandma, are you okay?"

Before Caroline could answer her, Josie strode across the room to confront the dark-haired man who was lounging against the wall. "I hope you're independently wealthy, Harper, because as of now, you're officially unemployable."

"Joselyn Galloway!" Caroline scolded. "What's gotten into you? Locke didn't empty my purse. *I* did."

Josie turned toward the woman in confused disbelief. "What?"

"I can't find my lipstick. You know how that can be. I feel like a frump without it." Caroline's tone took a wheedling turn. "Could I borrow yours?"

"Lipstick?"

"Not too red but not too pink either, if possible. I'm a little flushed as it is, what with all the excitement."

Josie needed to regain ground, and so she resisted an impulse to strangle Caroline. Instead, she moved to the older woman's side and draped an arm around her slender shoulders. "Anyone would be flushed and confused after being dragged down here like a common criminal." Raising her eyes to the agent's, she added quietly, "I hope you have a legitimate reason for questioning this woman, Harper."

For the first time, she was able to take a good look at him and saw that he was straight out of the official FBI coloring book—dark hair, steely eyes, gray suit, strong jaw, excellent build, and no-nonsense expression. She'd met a couple of these guys in her time, and of course had seen dozens of them in movies. No surprises here, thank goodness. He'd be easy to handle.

Agent Harper's voice was predictably calm and forthright. "This is a routine matter, Ms. Galloway. I stopped by your grandmother's house to ask a few nonobtrusive questions, but she said she'd feel more comfortable here. With you present. And so I accommodated her wishes."

"He didn't read me my rights, Josie," Caroline interrupted. "But I insisted on calling you anyway."

"I didn't read you your rights because you're not a suspect," Harper reminded her with a patient smile. "I've explained that—"

"I'll be the judge of my client's rights," Josie informed him briskly. "I'd like a few minutes alone with her now."

"Take all the time you want." Harper nodded. "Caroline, would you like me to track down that tea while you're visiting with your granddaughter?"

Josie's eyes narrowed at his use of the term "visit." Plus, where did he get off calling her client by her first name! "This isn't a social call, Agent Harper. I suggest you remember that."

"Josie!" Caroline turned to the man and sighed. "I'm so sorry, Locke. I didn't realize she'd react this way. I'll explain it all to her while you get the tea. And coffee for Josie, please."

Harper flashed his first smile, and it was a deadly one. "Cream? Sugar? Honey?"

"Cream for Josie, and a little lemon for me, thanks."

"Grandma . . ." Josie shook her sunstreaked curls in exasperated confusion. "Didn't your message say you were refusing to talk until you'd consulted with your attorney?"

"Yes."

"Then stop talking to Agent Harper. Let him go away for a few minutes so I can do my job. Please?"

Caroline smiled sweetly. "Of course. Locke? You'd better forget the refreshments for now."

"Whatever you say." Patting Caroline's shoulder as he passed her, he added mischievously, "I'll be right outside if you need me."

Josie waited in silence until the door had closed behind him, then muttered, "Thanks for making me look like a complete fool, Grandma."

"Don't be silly. You look lovely. Is that the blouse I gave you for Christmas? It brings out the green in your eyes, just like I said it would. I hope Locke noticed."

"You hope . . . ?" Josie sank into a chair and groaned as the true purpose of this little get-together came into sharp focus. After all her protests and warnings, her grandmother was still trying to set her up with every hunky guy she met! It was unbelievable. "You dragged an FBI agent down here just to meet me?"

"Don't be silly. He came to the house, but I don't allow strange men to just walk into my living room. And so I suggested we come here. I needed to come downtown anyway," she added defensively. "The Midsummer Madness sale started today, and I was about to call a taxi when Locke showed up on my doorstep. It was kismet."

Josie had to smile at that. And she had to admit that as frustrating as the situation had become, it was wonderful to see Caroline having so much fun. The radiance in her smile was worth a little inconvenience and embarrassment. Of course, inconveniencing the FBI seemed a bit presumptuous, even for Caroline, but to Locke Harper's credit, he was graciously playing along with the innocent manipulations.

"Listen, Grandma. I ran into Pete Hanover outside,

and he told me you witnessed a robbery. What's that all about?"

Caroline shrugged. "It was so long ago. On my honeymoon, in fact. I can barely remember it at all, so I doubt I can be much use to Locke—"

"On your *honeymoon*? You mean, like—fifty years ago?"

"Almost."

"Good grief. I can't believe the feds are wasting time and resources on some ancient crime. What exactly did Agent Harper tell you?"

Caroline pursed her lips. "Apparently, they never solved the crime. The file was inactive for the longest time, then mysteriously, some of the stolen jewels started showing up. The robber must have thought no one would notice, but Locke says these pieces are so distinctive, they attract attention even now. Isn't that remarkable?"

Josie shrugged. "Shouldn't these guys be trying to find serial killers and mad bombers instead of bothering old—I mean, senior citizens?"

"He hasn't been bothering me. He's been charming and attentive. Once you get to know him—"

"Reality check, Grandma. I'm *never* going to get to know him. He's obviously being a good sport about all this, but at some point it stops being cute and starts being obstruction of justice. Just tell me what you remember. If I don't see any problems, you can repeat it all to him, and that will be that."

"But, Josie—"

"I know what you're up to, Grandma, and it's not going to happen. For one thing, he's in the middle of an investigation. For another, I've sworn off cops. Remember?"

"He isn't a cop. He's an FBI agent. And he told me he's also an attorney, just like you. And he's handsome, don't you think?"

"I didn't notice."

Caroline's tone grew firm. "You were rude to him. I hope that's not what they taught you in law school. I'd hate to think my money paid for lessons in bad manners."

"It's called zealously defending my client, so let's get to it. Tell me what you remember about the robbery."

"It was so long ago. . . ."

Josie refused to let her stall. "You said it was on your honeymoon, so that was 1950, right? At a resort up along the coast. And the guy stole jewels? What else?"

"I don't remember much more, Josie. Do you think it's safe to talk to Locke about it?"

"Assuming you didn't do it," Josie teased, "and assuming you didn't withhold any information, then sure. Get it over with, so the guy can do his job. Shall I call him back in here?"

"Politely?"

"I'll be Little Miss Manners," Josie promised. "Then we'll go to the Midsummer Madness sale and get you something pretty to wear for the Fourth of July. Okay?"

"Are you sure you have time to shop?"

"I always have time for shopping," Josie assured her with a warm smile. "I inherited that particular chromosome from my grandma."

When Caroline's emerald eyes lit up with delight, Josie felt a familiar rush of affection and gratitude. She was so lucky to have someone like this in her life. The time they spent together, whether it was during their traditional Sunday dinner at Caroline's or an impromptu shopping spree or even a lame setup with an eligible bachelor, was precious to the adoring granddaughter.

Caroline Galloway had been nothing less than a rock for her grandchildren, especially when a horrifying tragedy had struck their family fifteen years earlier. Caroline had lost a husband and a son that day—and Josie had lost her father and her grandpa.

Josie's mother had been too distraught to handle the situation on her own and had gratefully accepted her mother-in-law's invitation to move into her house with her three young children. Together they had mourned and healed. Even when Josie's mother remarried and moved to San Diego with her younger children, Josie had stayed in Sutterville to finish high school. It was Caroline who sent her through college and law school and so, when it was time to establish a law practice, Josie had dutifully returned to northern California to make certain the older woman would never be lonely or neglected.

They looked out for one another, each in her own way, and although Caroline's way could be mindboggling when it came to the subject of prospective husbands for Josie, it had been a small price to pay for the gift of love and devotion.

"So, let's get this over with." Josie jumped to her feet and hurried toward the door. "No chitchat,

Grandma. Just answer his questions as simply and directly as possible. If something makes you uncomfortable, let me know, and I'll put a stop to it. Understand?"

"What about the lipstick?"

Groaning only slightly, the granddaughter reached into her briefcase and retrieved a mirror and a tube of Perfectly Pink lip gloss. "I know it used to be stylish to keep a guy waiting, Grandma, but—"

"I only need two minutes. In the rest room." Before Josie could protest, Caroline had brushed past her and opened the door. "I'll just be a minute, Locke. Get to know my granddaughter while I powder my nose."

The dark-haired agent, who had again been lounging against a wall, straightened and nodded respectfully. After Caroline disappeared around a corner, he turned and ambled casually toward Josie.

The fact that he was so relaxed about this matter was reassuring to the defense attorney. That, combined with the fact that this was a fifty-year-old unsolved case, was enough to convince her that Caroline was in no immediate danger from the federal government. Summoning another of her cordial yet distant smiles, she greeted him with a simple "Thanks for your patience. I promise we'll wrap this up soon."

"No problem." He pulled his shield from inside his suit jacket and moved to within inches of her. "We haven't actually been introduced. I'm Special Agent Locke Harper. I usually work out of Los Angeles, but this assignment is something of an aberration, as you've probably guessed. Anyway, we appreciate your cooperation. Joselyn Galloway, right?''

Josie stepped back slightly, unnerved by his sudden closeness. At six foot two—possibly three—he seemed to tower over her, yet his mouth was disturbingly close to the top of her head, so close that she could feel the warmth of his breath. Such intimate overtones, imagined or not, were simply unacceptable under the circumstances, and so she quickly regained her equilibrium and offered her hand for a brisk, no-nonsense handshake.

"We'll cooperate, but I should tell you up front that my grandmother doesn't remember much about the robbery. It's been forever, as you know. I assume that's why you call this an aberration? But we'll be happy to try to answer any reasonable questions."

"Fair enough." He seemed to be in no hurry to release her hand. "You have an interesting reputation around this place, Ms. Galloway.

Pulling free sharply from his grip, she scanned his face for a sign that he was mocking her. "They told you about the Parker case? What exactly did they say?"

"Enough to convince me that the guy's a menace to society. And thanks to you, he's back on the street."

"Thanks to me," she corrected him haughtily, "the Sutterville police force is more likely to read you your rights the next time they want to question you. That's my job, Harper. Protecting guys like you from guys like you. Is that a problem?"

"Not for me." A smile tugged at the corner of his

mouth. "Fortunately, your grandmother isn't a suspect in this case. Just a witness."

"Do you have a suspect?"

Locke shook his head. "We barely even have a lead, other than the fact that some of the contraband showed up in a pawnshop in Reno recently."

"And that's enough for the Bureau to give the case this kind of attention after all these years?"

"This case is very low priority," he corrected. "But I was headed up this way on vacation, so I volunteered to look into it. For personal reasons."

Josie's antennae went up almost instantly. Personal involvement on the part of the investigating officer was a complication in any case, federal or otherwise. Maybe this situation wasn't so casual after all. "Thanks for the warning."

"I meant it as an explanation, not a warning, but take it any way you want. I don't play games, Ms. Galloway. I'll be straight with you in this matter. You have my word. Plus"—the handsome smile returned—"I like your grandmother. She's extremely disarming."

"Well . . ." Josie glanced nervously down the corridor, hoping to catch sight of Caroline's return. Instead, Pete Hanover strode into view with an expression Josie recognized instantly. After a disastrous attempt at dating, followed by two years of wary friendship, they had learned one another's tricks only too well.

"I have a message for you, Harper." Pete handed the agent a folded piece of paper.

As he read the contents, Locke frowned slightly.

Then he raised his eyes to Josie's, and she saw for the first time that the unflappable agent could be annoyed. It was somehow reassuring—that is, until the reason for his annoyance was revealed. "Your grandmother went shopping."

"What?" Grabbing the note from his hand, she studied it in mortified disbelief. Caroline had, in fact, ditched them!

"Do I hear wedding bells?" Pete teased.

"Go away," Josie glared. "And try to grow up, will you? These stupid games—"

"Hey, don't blame the messenger." The detective laughed. "She's *your* client."

Josie turned to Locke and explained unhappily, "Please don't misunderstand this. It's not like she's trying to impede your investigation or anything. It's just that she's a hopeless matchmaker. I know that's the lamest excuse you've ever heard in your life, but it's true."

"Matchmaker?"

"I know—it's totally bizarre. But there's precedent, believe me. Anytime a single, nice-looking guy crosses her path—boom! She's off and running. I've been through this dozens of times, but this takes the cake, and I totally apologize." Struggling to regain some semblance of professional decorum, she added dramatically, "I take full responsibility for my client's behavior, of course. And I assure you she isn't hiding any information. If you give me a number where I can reach you, I'll locate her and we can set up another meeting at your convenience."

Taking the note from her hand, Locke tapped his

finger on the last line solemnly. "It says right here, the three of us are meeting tonight, at seven-thirty, at someplace called La Torta."

Josie felt a warm flush engulf her cheeks. "I'm so mortified. We'll meet at her house—"

"We have to eat," the agent interrupted gently. "Let her have her fun. As long as she answers a few questions for me, no harm done."

"That's extremely decent of you, Agent Harper. And"—Josie's jaw tightened in grim determination— "I guarantee you she'll be there, if I have to drag her there myself. Of course," she added wryly, "once I get her there, you may have to restrain her, so make sure you bring your handcuffs."

"Handcuffs are standard issue for a date with Josie," Pete Hanover added helpfully. When she whirled toward him in disgust, he backed away as though completely terrified. "Good luck tonight, Harper. You'll need it." His booming laughter echoed through the halls even after he'd disappeared from view, and Josie knew beyond a doubt that he was sharing the story with the rest of the force. And they, of course, were loving it.

"Now that my humiliation is complete, I guess I'll just grab my briefcase and slink away."

"For what it's worth, I think it's great that your grandmother cares so much about you," Locke soothed. "Don't give it another thought."

"Thanks." Smiling in true appreciation, she hastily took her leave before anything else could go wrong.

TWO

Josie eased her vintage Mustang convertible into a parking space behind La Torta, then reached across to the passenger seat and took her grandmother's hand in her own. "Before we go inside, let's have a game plan. Okay?"

"My game plan is to tell the FBI the truth," Caroline replied.

"Whatever. The point is, as much as you might want Harper and I to dance and all that, this is a business meeting. Understood?"

"Yes."

Reclining her seat a bit, Josie admitted, "I'm a little freaked out by all this, Grandma. I mean, fun is fun, but we're talking about the Federal Bureau of Investigation here. We don't want to push our luck. And so"—she took a deep breath—"I'm willing to make a deal with you."

"A deal?"

"That's right. You're always bugging me to go out with your friend Selma's nephew. So, as much as it pains me to do this, I absolutely promise that if you cooperate with Harper tonight, and drop the match-making, I'll go out with the cook."

"He isn't a cook. He's a chef."

"Whatever. I'll get naked with him if you cooperate with the FBI."

"Joselyn Galloway!" Caroline laughed lightly. "Tell me the truth. Don't you think Locke is adorable?"

"Men with guns are never adorable. And that bulge you noticed under his clothes was definitely a gun."

"Joselyn!"

Josie grinned. "He's handsome. He's also FBI. Which usually stands for fastidious, boring, and interchangeable."

"What does that mean?"

"It means they're all alike. This guy," she added softly, "would give his life for you. Because you're a citizen of the United States, and he's your servant. He's squeaky clean and perfect to the core. Perfection," she added melodramatically, "does *not* turn me on. Plus . . ." She dropped the bantering tone. "He says he has a personal interest in solving this case. I've seen that kind of thing before, Grandma. I saw it with Pete when his girlfriend was threatened by a stalker. It was almost a disaster. Every time cops get personal, things get complicated."

"I don't understand."

Josie pursed her lips. "Okay, let's put it this way. Locke Harper can't afford to like us. Not you, and not me. Because for some reason he needs to solve this case at any price."

Caroline considered this for a long moment. "But you do think he's cute?"

"I think he's darling. If I hadn't sworn off cops, and if he wasn't taking this thing personally, I definitely would let you set me up with him."

Caroline smiled impishly. "I think that's the closest I've ever come to succeeding with one of my blind-date attempts." Her green eyes darkened as she added almost plaintively, "I can't stand seeing you alone, Josie. You bring such joy to me, and you'd be such a wonderful mother—"

"That's it! Case closed. We cooperate with the FBI, I go out with the cook, and we're even. Agreed?"

"Agreed."

"And you'll answer all Harper's questions unless one of us gives the other a signal."

Caroline was clearly intrigued. "What signal?"

"If I'm bothered, or you're bothered, we'll say we need to powder our noses, or whatever. Then we'll both go to the rest room and plan a new strategy. But for now," she added quietly, "our strategy is honesty. Just answer his questions. Okay?"

Josie hadn't changed her outfit. The modest black suit and green silk blouse had seemed perfect for a business dinner. For some reason, however, Agent Locke Harper had shed his gray suit in favor of a black polo shirt and black jeans.

Because he's on vacation, Josie reminded herself weakly. *And that's how hunks-on-vacation dress.* She would have given anything to be able to turn back time and arrive at La Torta in her new red tube dress. What a burn!

"You have to order cheese enchiladas and a strawberry margarita," Caroline was instructing the agent cheerfully. "That's what all the young people order."

Locke Harper smiled. "Could I get a beer instead?"

"My husband drank beer." Caroline beamed.

"Kismet again," Josie observed sourly, then looked up at the expectant waiter and announced, "We'll all have cheese enchiladas. Plus, bring us one beer, one margarita, and one black coffee."

"*Bueno.*" The waiter bowed slightly and hurried away.

"Okay, let's get down to business. Agent Harper—"

"Call him Locke," Caroline interrupted firmly.

"Fine. Locke? Did you want to ask my grandmother some questions?"

The agent nodded. "Let me begin by saying: This is not an interrogation. You were already interviewed, years ago, and I've read your account of the circumstances. Now that time has passed and things aren't as tumultuous as they were back then, I just wanted to know if you remembered anything else—no matter how insignificant it might seem to you."

"I love this song," Caroline sighed. Turning to Josie, she added, "Your grandfather and I used to dance to this. What's it called?"

"It's called 'Spend the Rest of Your Life in the Slammer if You Don't Cooperate,'" Josie grumbled.

"It's called 'Smoke Gets In Your Eyes'," Locke corrected with a chuckle. "Did you dance to this music at the mansion on the night of the robbery, Caroline?"

Josie frowned. "What mansion?"

"In those days the honeymoon cottages at Driftwood Point were near to, but not under common ownership with, a huge summer home owned by the Greybill family," Locke explained. "You've heard of them, right?"

"Massively rich, and they run for office from time to time but lose?"

"That's them. Anyway, Caroline and your grandfather were honeymooning in one of the cottages, but the actual crimes took place in the mansion."

"Oh?" Josie gave her grandmother a pointed scowl. "You didn't mention that."

"We honeymooned at the cottages," Caroline confirmed. "The Greybills didn't matter to us, and vice versa. But they invited all the newlyweds to a party on the Fourth of July. To watch fireworks and all that. Mr. Greybill was robbed—and killed—at the mansion."

"Killed?" Josie gasped. "I thought you were investigating a simple robbery."

"I don't think I ever said that," Locke replied evenly.

"Does it matter?" Caroline interrupted.

Josie took a deep breath. "The statute of limitations on robbery has long since passed. Which is a fancy way of saying they can no longer prosecute the robber. But there's no statute of limitations for murder."

"Oh, dear."

Josie looked deep into Locke Harper's cool blue eyes and demanded, "Is this a murder investigation?"

"Yes."

She felt so stupid. So naive and gullible. He had said it was personal. The FBI had authorized an investigation. Yet they had all been treating it like some sort of parlor game. Apparently, when Locke Harper said he was being straight with a person, he meant only to the extent that that person was competent. And Josie had been woefully incompetent.

She almost spat her next question. "Is my grandmother a suspect?"

"Of course not. She was the only eyewitness, which means I need her input. But no, she wasn't a suspect then, and she's not a suspect now. I give you my word."

"Grandma?" Josie demanded. "Did you witness a robbery *and* a murder?"

Caroline shrugged. "I was an *ear*witness, not an eyewitness. I heard struggling. That's all I know."

Locke studied her carefully. "That's consistent with the agent's notes at the time. You haven't remembered anything else since then?"

"No."

"I see." He was clearly disappointed. "I guess that's that."

"I might be able to remember more if only . . ." Caroline sighed loudly. "Oh, well."

"If only what, Grandma?" Josie demanded.

"If only I could go back there. To the scene of the crime. I almost feel I have information buried in my subconscious, but I can't get ahold of it. Does that make sense?"

Locke said "Yes" at the very instant Josie said "No." The waiter, who had chosen that moment to bring their drinks, murmured something unintelligible and hurried away just as the granddaughter added tartly, "You think you have information but you can't get hold of it? That's nuts, Grandma."

"Actually . . ." Locke studied Caroline intently. "That's exactly what I was hoping to hear." Turning to Josie, he explained patiently, "I could tell from the original agent's notes that your grandmother was distressed at the time. She was blocking the whole experience because it scared her. Which," he added quickly, "is absolutely normal. But it's been years now. The situation is less threatening."

Caroline nodded emphatically. "I'm not scared anymore. I *want* to remember. If only we could— what's the word?—facilitate it."

Josie had watched Locke's expression go from guarded to almost victorious. Now he suggested excitedly, "Would you consent to hypnosis? We've had incredible results with it."

"Hold on!" Josie blurted. "You're not hypnotizing my—my client. No way. Not until you've told me everything there is to know about this case."

Locke's cobalt eyes grew dark. "I'm sure Caroline doesn't have anything to hide."

She almost thanked him then, for taking this out of the realm of semisocial and returning it to the dangerous world of official investigation—a world in which she had learned to thrive. "This interview is over. I'm sorry if we inconvenienced you, Agent Harper, but I think it's best if you leave. Right now."

"Joselyn Galloway!" Carolyn gasped. "What on earth are you doing? Locke is my guest tonight."

Turning to the agent, she pleaded, "Don't go yet. When I said you could 'facilitate' my memory, I wasn't talking about hypnosis. I was talking about— well, about returning to the scene of the crime, like I said before." When they both stared at her in wonder, the older woman explained brightly, "I think I could remember if only I could go back to the mansion. Relive that night and the crime. Doesn't that make sense?"

Josie could actually feel the room spinning around her. She wasn't sure who was more obnoxious, the agent who took this murder investigation "personally," or the witness who wanted to turn it into *Murder on the Orient Express!* As a granddaughter, Josie might have been able to muddle through this, but as Caroline Galloway's attorney, she had to act decisively.

Turning to the agent, she announced as confidently as she could, "My client has made herself clear. She has nothing to add at this time. She may or may not remember something in the future, and if she does, I give you my word that I'll contact you immediately."

"I said no such thing," Carolyn reprimanded. "I'm so sorry, Locke. Please forgive my granddaughter."

Locke took a long, slow drink of beer, directly from the bottle, before admitting, "I'm a little confused myself, Caroline. Are you saying you want me to take you to the scene of the crime? To Driftwood Point?"

The older woman nodded. "You said you have a reservation there this week, so I assumed Josie and I could just tag along with you. Was I being presumptuous?"

"Grandma!"

Caroline turned to her granddaughter and scolded, "You haven't had a vacation since you graduated from law school! The three of us could go up there and solve this crime once and for all, and it would be a wonderful use of a week. I think it's stubborn and unattractive of you to resist the idea."

"Stubborn and unattractive? Unattractive to whom? *Him?*" Josie glared. "Are you nuts?"

Caroline stood up—regal and haughty—and informed them proudly, "I'm taking a taxi home. Don't bother to follow me. I want you two to work this out between yourselves."

When Josie tried to object, suggesting instead that this was a good time to "powder their noses," Caroline silenced her with an imperious glare. "I give you my word that I will abide by your decision."

Josie's eyed her skeptically. "What does *that* mean?"

"It means, young lady, that if you and Locke decide there's no use in the three of us going to Driftwood Point, fine. I'm just an old woman trying to do the right thing."

You're an old woman trying to set me up with a hunky guy, Josie wanted to retort, but her grandmother's expression was uncharacteristically serious, and so she remained silent in spite of herself.

"I'm going to have the waiter hail me a taxi, and then I'm going home. Call me tomorrow with the decision."

"Grandma—"

"That's final, Joselyn. Locke, if we don't meet again, it was lovely knowing you. Good evening."

They stared in chagrined disbelief as she stormed away, then Josie assured the agent nervously, "It's the matchmaking thing again. This is all part of a lame attempt to get us alone together."

"But it can't be good for her heart."

Josie almost smiled at the misplaced concern. "Don't let that dainty exterior fool you. She's as strong as an ox."

"Then why does she . . . ?" His gaze dropped to his plate. "Never mind. I'm sure you know what you're doing."

It was the longest silence Josie could remember. Maybe, if she hadn't blocked all memories of her father's plane crash, this moment might have some serious competition, but as it was, this was it. 'Good for her heart?' *Grandma's* heart? What did the FBI know that Josie didn't?

"You investigated her?" Josie whispered finally. "Good grief, Harper, is she okay?"

Abject apology shone in his eyes. "I don't have the details. I ran a financial on her—for obvious reasons—and the prescription kept coming up—"

"Heart medicine?" Josie demanded frantically. "That's crazy. Did you take a good look at her? She's the picture of health! I mean, she's a little pale, but—" The reality of his statement began to penetrate her brain. "What are you saying?"

"She looks healthy," he agreed carefully. "With proper medication, these conditions—"

"Conditions! She has a condition?" Josie buried her face in her hands, destroyed by the fact that her grandmother had not confided to her in her hour of need. And why hadn't Josie *noticed*? Dinner every Sunday, outings almost every week, yet Josie hadn't taken the time to actually *look* at the woman? To see that the capable workhorse who had raised two generations of Galloways had grown frail beyond her years?

"Don't beat yourself up over it," Locke was insisting gallantly. "She looks great, just like you said. I would never have guessed if I hadn't seen her bills."

A light, dim but noticeable, went on in Josie's head. "Her bills? You checked her finances because—because you wanted to see if she had any influxes of cash at the same time the jewels were pawned?"

Locke flushed. "You're pretty sharp. But believe me, I never really suspected her. I just had to know before I came here. Does that make any sense at all?"

"Nothing makes sense," Josie said quietly. "Nothing at all. My world makes no sense. It's as simple as that."

"Do you want me to go?"

It took a moment for the question to register, then she shook her head. "It's not your fault. In fact, you've made her happier than I've seen her in months. You should feel good about yourself."

"So should you. You're the light of her life," Locke assured her. "I feel like a jerk for springing this on you—"

"Don't." She caught and held his gaze. "I had to

know. And I'm eternally grateful to you for giving me the information. I just wish . . ."

"So do I."

They were quiet for what seemed like forever, then Locke ventured cautiously, "Would you consider coming to Driftwood Point with me? I mean, the three of us. Like Caroline said, I have a reservation at the cottages. Maybe the trip would do her—and you—some good. And obviously it would help me out."

"Because . . ." She studied him intently. "You need to solve this case for personal reasons, and Grandma's the key."

"Right."

"So? Tell me why it's personal."

"Would you like to dance?"

"Excuse me?"

He inclined his head toward the dance floor. "I'm going to tell you something personal. I'd rather do that on the dance floor, where I know you can't see my face."

"Good grief." Folding her napkin carefully, she mentally prepared herself. She was about to dance with an incredibly attractive guy, but there would be no joy in it, because her grandmother was dying, and because her dance partner was going to whisper dark secrets, rather than sweet nothings, into her ear.

It was one of Josie's favorite songs. A slow, seductive instrumental version of "Breaking Up Is Hard to Do." Breaking up *was* hard. She had done it often enough—usually because she was dating a cop/cowboy/captain who was absolutely wrong for her. She wondered briefly, as Locke Harper took her into his strong arms, if he'd had half as many breakups as she. If so, she was pretty certain he'd been the dumper rather than the dumpee. He was such a perfect physical specimen, a female would have had to be mad to kick him out of her bed!

Rock solid was the only way to describe his muscular body. There was no excess—only lean, mean power. Despite that, he held her gently, as though she were a fragile maiden rather than a tough criminal defense attorney. It was nice. False, but nice.

"Talk to me," she whispered into his chest. "Tell me why the case is personal."

He cleared his throat audibly, then confided, "My grandfather on my mother's side was the agent in charge of that case."

Josie pulled away slightly, just enough to allow her to gaze up at him in amazement. "Really?"

His smile was rueful. "It was one of his first assignments. And this case—the unsolved robbery and homicide—made him realize the Bureau wasn't for him. Don't look so sad," he added quickly. "After he left the Bureau, he became a federal district judge and eventually sat on the Court of Appeals. He loved his life and his career."

Josie melted against the agent, grateful for the respite from unhappy endings. "The case went unsolved, so now you want to solve it as a tribute to your grandfather? You're using your vacation to do it because the Bureau couldn't care less. Right?"

"More or less. So," he added self-consciously, "the

next time you think your situation is lame, remember me. This one beats them all."

"I think it's sweet," she enthused. "Does he know you're doing it, or are you going to surprise him?"

"He passed away two years ago."

"Oh, I'm so sorry."

"Don't be. I think he'll know. Don't you?"

"Sure he will." She leaned her cheek against his chest. "Now I wish Grandma really knew something that might help you."

"I think maybe she does."

Josie pulled back again, staring up at him with a mixture of confusion and suspicion. "What does *that* mean?"

The song was ending, and Locke took the opportunity to suggest they return to the table.

Josie agreed immediately. This wasn't a conversation she wanted to have in his arms. "You think Grandma is holding out on you?"

"Intentionally? No way," Locke assured her as he ushered her into her chair. "I think the information is buried in her subconscious."

She remembered his hypnosis suggestion and shook her head in warning. "I'd never allow the prosecution to hypnotize a client. Plus, she has . . . she has a heart condition. It's not an option, Harper. I'm sorry. I think it's sweet that you want to vindicate your grandfather, but you'll have to find another way."

Locke nodded confidently. "Caroline herself suggested another way." When Josie simply frowned in confusion, he explained, "She should return to the scene of the crime. To refresh her memory. I can question her there, and she may remember something crucial."

Josie lowered her gaze, unwilling to disappoint him directly. "You're forgetting something. When your grandfather questioned her originally, she was *at* the scene of the crime. If it didn't work then, how would it work fifty years later?"

"That's the point," Locke confided impatiently. "Grandfather *didn't* question her properly. He couldn't. He was too—well, too taken with her."

"Excuse me?"

The agent's jaw tightened visibly. "I know it sounds crazy, but I've read his notes. All his files on the case. He couldn't bring himself to interrogate Caroline because he had a massive crush on her. I know it sounds crazy—"

"It does," Josie interrupted gleefully. "It's totally crazy and completely mortifying for you, and I'm *so relieved,* because now we're even." Her voice bubbled with delight. "Grandma embarrassed me by the matchmaking, and your grandfather embarrassed you because he was so lovestruck by Grandma that he couldn't think straight! I love it!"

"Lovestruck?" Locke grinned sheepishly. "That's the perfect word for it. One look into her big green eyes and he was toast. If his notes are any indication of his condition, he was just this side of a babbling idiot."

"Wow."

"Yeah, wow."

Josie couldn't stop smiling. How romantic could it

get? A serious young agent sent to investigate a grisly murder but blindsided and lovestruck instead by a golden-haired, emerald-eyed bride in distress!

"Did he look like you?" she asked without thinking.

Locke smiled. "Not at all. But according to the notes, you and Caroline are a matched set."

"That's what they say," Josie blushed. "Of course, in temperament we're eons apart. It's nice, though, that he mentioned her eyes in his notes. She and I always think of them as our best feature."

Locke nodded. "They're lethal weapons, beyond a doubt. My grandfather couldn't get past them. He couldn't do his job. The bottom line is that even though your grandmother was an eyewitness—"

"*Ear*witness."

"Right. Even though she was an *ear*witness, she wasn't thoroughly and professionally questioned, and so valuable clues may never have been uncovered."

Josie sighed and rested her elbows on the table, chin in hands. "Are you loving this half as much as I am?"

"Probably not," Locke admitted. "I want to solve the crime. Grandfather could have solved it himself easily if he hadn't been so—what was your word?"

"Lovestruck."

"Precisely. I'd like to set that straight for him."

Josie reached across the table to pat his hand. "I'd love to help, big fella, but no one hypnotizes my clients. *Or* my family members. Aren't there any other witnesses you can hound?"

He chuckled self-consciously. "If there were, I

would have run screaming out of Sutterville hours ago. But the truth is, Caroline Galloway is my only hope."

"Caroline Galloway," Josie reminded him sadly, "has a bad heart."

Locke nodded. "On the other hand, there's a fifty-thousand-dollar reward for information leading to the recovery of the jewels. Maybe easing Caroline's financial problems would help her heart condition in the long run."

"Grandma doesn't have any financial problems," Josie corrected. "She's loaded. The woman sent me through law school without even—" Her stomach turned ominously and she pleaded, as softly as she dared, "Oh, no. Don't do this to me again."

"I thought you knew," he apologized. "The situation is so—well, it's so precarious, frankly. If she loses that house—"

Josie's gasp of dismay silenced him and he reached shakily for his beer. "Sorry, Josie. I didn't mean for any of this to happen. I just assumed . . ."

"You just assumed," she finished sadly, "that a good granddaughter would take the time to notice these things. Grandma's poverty stricken and dying, and I'm completely oblivious to it. I hate myself!"

"She should never have kept it from you," he protested loyally. "Anyone can see how dedicated you are to her. She should have asked for your help months ago. As it is—"

"As it is, she's going to lose the house?" Josie whispered. "She'll never be able to bear that, Locke. I mean, if she sold it, fine. She's not a materialist or anything. But to lose it—to have a bank take it from her—would be horrible. She's so proud. Too proud." Josie bit her lip. "Is there really a fifty-thousand-dollar reward?"

"Absolutely. All I have to do is solve the case, and Caroline can have every penny. Let me hypnotize her—"

"That's not necessary," Josie interrupted. "All we have to do is go to Driftwood Point, and she'll spill all the details."

"What?"

"Don't let her con you. Return to the scene of the crime? That's a matchmaking tactic. She wants to get us alone at a honeymoon spot on the Fourth of July and wait for the fireworks to start. Vintage Grandma." Josie smiled ruefully. "She's tricky but she's not cruel. She wouldn't suggest going there without knowing that there's something she can tell you. Something she didn't tell your grandfather. I can almost promise you that."

"So? If we go there, she'll tell me?" Locke grinned in relief. "That's great! And you don't even have to be involved if you don't want to. I'll take her there myself—she'll be in good hands, believe me—"

"Time out! *I'm* the one you're being matched with, remember? What makes you think she'll go without me?"

Locke shrugged. "I'll tell her about the reward."

"Don't you dare!" Josie lowered her voice and added sweetly, "If you tell her you know about her poverty, she'll be mortified. And if she suspects that you told *me,* she'll be destroyed. We have to let her get the reward without letting her know we know she needs it.''

"You just lost me.''

Josie reached across the table again, taking his huge hand in her own. ''She's a proud woman, Locke. And a matchmaker to the core. We'll let her think her little scheme is working. The three of us will go to the beach; you and I will pretend to be falling for each other; and Grandma will mysteriously remember details that will lead to the apprehension of the robber, *et voilà!* Case closed. Mortgage paid off. Everyone lives happily ever after.'' With a warning glare she added, ''Do you want to solve this stupid crime or not?''

"I still don't see why we can't just be honest with her.''

Perched on the hood of her Mustang in the restaurant parking lot, Josie gave her reluctant co-conspirator a look of disgust. ''We've been over it five times. Can't we just call it a night? If we're all going to drive five hours up the coast tomorrow—''

"You're sure she'll agree?''

Josie shrugged. ''It was her idea, remember?''

"And you can take the time off? What about your clients?''

"My clients are behaving themselves for the time being, which means I have no pressing court appearances. It also means I have no income at the moment. Luckily, I have enough from tax time to tide me over.''

"You do taxes?"

"Sure. It pays more dependably than criminal defense. Ergo, summer is a good time for me to take a vacation at the beach with a dashing FBI agent."

"Flattery will get you nowhere," he warned. "Why not try honesty instead. For the novelty, if nothing else. If you tell her about the fifty thousand, she'll be happy. Right?"

"Momentarily. And then if we *don't* solve the stupid crime, she'll be disappointed. And embarrassed."

"So what? At some point it has to be dealt with—"

"Maybe not! That's the point. If we solve the case and she gets the fifty thousand, we can sweep it under the rug forever." Sliding off the hood, she moved to stand before him. "That's how we do things in our family, Locke, and it works really well. Don't interfere. Just help."

He was shaking his head again. "I don't like lying to her."

"Do you want to solve this as a tribute to your grandfather or not?"

"It's not that simple."

"Sure it is. Haven't you ever worked under cover?"

"Is that an invitation?" he teased.

"That's the spirit." She grinned. "If Grandma thinks we're flirting with each other, she'll easily believe the rest of the story."

"The lie."

"Whatever. The point is, she knows I never take vacations. If I take this one with you, it's for one of two reasons. The reward, which is a secret. Or the fact that I'm completely lovestruck by you—which is the perfect cover."

For the first time, he seemed intrigued by the idea. "Am I lovestruck too?"

"That's optional. You already have a good reason to go on the trip, so you don't need to be lovestruck. If you want, you can be all business." Josie moistened her lips, then plotted out loud. "Grandma will like it either way. If we're both lovey-dovey, it'll be sweet. If you resist my advances, it'll be dramatic."

Her voice grew rich with excitement. "Actually, that's the perfect choice. I try my darnedest to seduce you, but you resist. Eventually, of course, you succumb to my charms. She'll *love* it."

"This is crazy."

"Are you engaged or anything like that?"

"No."

"Then what's the problem?"

He chuckled in defeat. "There is no problem?"

"Exactly. Pick us up at nine A.M. sharp. At Grandma's house. And try to look sexy, please. It'll make my job easier."

"I'm sorry if I upset you or embarrassed you, Josie. I guess I wasn't thinking straight. He just seemed like such a perfect gentleman, through and through. That's all I really want for you."

Josie studied her grandmother fondly. "That's all I want for me too—a perfect man. Unfortunately, they don't exist. Still"—she eyed the woman carefully—"I'll admit Locke's about as close as they get.

He's *sooo* attractive. For two cents I'd close up the office for a week and let him whisk you and me off to honeymoonland for a romantic rendezvous.''

Caroline stared in delight. "You really like him that much?"

"I'm afraid so. The guy's gorgeous. You totally picked a winner for once."

Caroline sipped her tea. "I knew I saw sparks flying. You should ask him to dinner and cook him something delicious. That's the way to a man's heart, you know."

Guilt stricken at the mention of *anyone's* heart, Josie murmured, "It's not that easy. He's all business. He'll leave for Driftwood Point tomorrow with or without us. If only he weren't so obsessed with solving the case."

Caroline bit her lip, then reached for her pocketbook and pulled out a coin purse. "Here—two shiny pennies. You said for two cents you'd go to Driftwood Point with us, so do it." Before Josie could respond, the older woman pleaded, "Won't you just put yourself first for once in your life? You're always worrying about me or about your clients. In the meantime, life is passing you by. If you think Locke might be the one—"

"The one?" Josie flushed. "I never said that, Grandma. I just said he's attractive—"

"Fine! Then have an affair with him," Caroline blurted. "Not that I approve of such things. But in your case it's better than nothing. I know for a fact that you haven't allowed a man to make—well, to make you feel good about yourself—in months. If

Locke can make you happy, even for a week, why not let him?"

Josie's blush deepened. For Caroline—a staunch proponent of "waiting for the wedding night"—that was quite a suggestion. "It's tempting."

"Then do it! I know you're resisting him because he's a law enforcement officer, but let's face facts, Josie. That's what you like. When you were a girl, you loved cowboys and soldiers. When you opened your law practice, it was suddenly detectives and deputies. It's your destiny to like such men."

"Unfortunately," Josie murmured, "it's not a two-way street. Guys like that don't want women like me. They want to be in control—to protect the helpless. I'm not helpless, and I don't let anyone control me."

"Maybe Locke's different."

"He's different, all right." Josie laughed lightly. "I have a feeling we'd be surprised if we knew all of his secrets."

"That's funny." Caroline smiled. "I like him because he's not the type to *have* secrets. He seems so straightforward and honest." Her emerald eyes began to twinkle. "Did he kiss you tonight?"

"I told you, he's obsessed with the case. If I want to catch his eye, I'll need to bat my eyelashes and show some serious cleavage. I guess I'd better take my new red dress to Driftwood Point."

"Does that mean we're going? Oh, how exciting!"

Josie winced at the thought that the woman might become overly stimulated. What would it do to her heart? "Take it easy, Grandma," she warned nervously. "I'm not promising anything in the romance department. He's all business, remember?"

"Just be yourself," Caroline counseled proudly. "Who could resist that for long?"

THREE

As Locke transferred his luggage from the sedan he had originally rented for the trip to the shiny black four-wheel-drive powerhouse that seemed better suited to transporting a party of three to a week at the beach, he mentally prepared himself for his bizarre passengers. Not that he didn't like them, each in her own way. It was just that he had learned in less than a day that they were both manipulative and unpredictable. If he wasn't careful, his agenda for this trip would be lost in a whirlwind of confused motives, little white lies, and misplaced good intentions.

First there was Caroline, pretending to cooperate in his investigation as a means of setting him up with her granddaughter. Then there was the granddaughter, pretending to cooperate with the setup in order to recover the reward money. And somehow, Locke had agreed to pretend to resist the setup, and pretend to be ignorant of the reward money, if he had any hope at all of succeeding in his investigation. As though these manipulations weren't enough, there were undercurrents—Caroline's heart condition, for one, and Josie's suspicious nature, for another.

And Locke was not completely innocent either. What about *his* hidden agenda? He had told Josie about his grandfather's involvement in the original investigation but had allowed her to believe he was solving the case as a tribute to the old guy. "Tribute," he knew, was probably the wrong word. "Vindication" might be a better characterization of his intentions.

The bottom line was he had come to Sutterville with little hope of actually learning something new from Caroline Galloway after all these years. He had believed her to be what his grandfather had seen: a naive young bride terrified by having witnessed a robbery/murder and unable to cooperate despite her fervent desire to do so. Now that he had seen Caroline in action, he suspected instead that she had manipulated his grandfather into backing off on the questioning. She had used tears and trembling to appeal to the protector in him, undermining his ability to do his job.

Before Locke hoisted the last piece of luggage—his grandfather's worn leather briefcase—into the back compartment, he took a moment to remember its contents. Pages and pages of handwritten notes detailing the first few hours of scrutinizing the Driftwood Point crime scene and interrogating the partygoers, who had apparently heard and seen nothing due to the fireworks display and live orchestra. More than anything, those notes described the complete breakdown of discipline on the part of an investigator.

Seduced, subverted and rendered completely ineffective—an agent's worst nightmare. It had destroyed his grandfather's confidence—Locke was certain of that. And it had planted a seed of doubt in Locke's own self-image. Somehow, solving the case, even at this late date, would put things right again.

Setting the briefcase carefully into place, Locke glanced at his watch and had to smile. Ten minutes to nine. Across town, another professional was undoubtedly going over a last-minute game plan, anxious to make no mistakes. There was a lot at stake in this for Joselyn Galloway too, and so she would try to manipulate Locke. Of that he had no doubt. And Caroline would work him over too, for purposes known and unknown.

In a way, this would actually be a total vindication of his grandfather's downfall. Locke had hoped only to solve the case, but it seemed he was getting a chance to do much more—to prove, once and for all, that big green eyes, breathless entreaties, and other assorted feminine ploys could not subvert a highly disciplined Special Agent of the Federal Bureau of Investigation—the quintessential law enforcement officer of the most powerful country on earth!—from doing what he was trained to do.

"What a beautiful car," Caroline Galloway was enthusing minutes later. "Or is it a truck?"

"It's gorgeous," Josie confirmed. "Nice touch, Harper. You're spoiling us."

"Here, let me get that suitcase for you," Locke offered.

Instinctively bristling at the condescending attitude, Josie assured him, "I've got it," and heaved her bag easily into the back of the vehicle. Then she remembered she was supposed to be throwing herself at the dark-haired agent and smiled ruefully. It was not going to come easy to her—not after a lifetime of constantly proving she could take care of herself.

Still, she had done her best for the occasion, wearing a skimpy pink halter top and tight faded jeans, and curling her sunstreaked hair so that it bounced playfully about her shoulders. Grandma had approved the look instantly but had spritzed her granddaughter's bare, tanned shoulders with Chanel No. 5 as added insurance just moments before Locke pulled up in his fancy male fantasy-mobile. Second only to guns, Josie knew how these guys loved their rides. So predictable!

She noticed that he had followed her suggestion to wear something sexy, namely faded jeans, along with a loose black and gold Pittsburgh Steelers football jersey. It was a tribute to his broad shoulders and tight abdominals that he didn't need to wear a tight shirt to remind anyone how fit and muscular he was.

Predictably, Grandma the matchmaker insisted on sitting in the backseat. "Studies have shown it's the safest spot," she informed Josie briskly. "And I plan on sleeping most of the way. I was so excited last night, thinking about this lovely outing, I could barely close my eyes."

Locke quickly demonstrated the many luxurious features of the vehicle. Not only could any passenger fully recline at the touch of a button, but most of the captain-style seats swiveled. "So even if Josie sits up front, you two can play cards or visit easily. Of course"—he pretended to glare at Josie—"your primary duty is to navigate. I've never driven up the coast before."

When the last of Caroline's cases had been loaded, Josie suggested hopefully, "Would you like me to drive, Locke? I've never actually taken the cutoff to Driftwood Point, but I've driven the whole coast from San Francisco all the way up to Crescent City. Plus"— she grinned mischievously—"I can't wait to see what this baby can do. It must have a jillion horsepower."

"More or less, which is why *I'm* driving. Get used to taking orders, counselor. There can be only one leader on an adventure like this, and it's going to be me."

She studied him warily. Was he going to do this the whole trip? Take advantage of her? Knowing that her undercover role was to pretend to be enamored of him? And, of course, he could do whatever he liked, because she had stupidly allowed him to assume the role of businesslike lawman, impervious to the charms of the female who shamelessly adored him. What had she been thinking?

As soon as Grandma's asleep, we're going to rewrite this script, Mr. Bigshot, she warned him silently. Then she sighed, remembering the reason she was putting herself through this humiliation. If taking orders from the FBI for a couple of days would give Grandma some financial security and peace of mind, Josie wasn't about to complain. At least, not too much.

Summoning all the love she had for the older

woman, Josie stepped close to the federal agent and
cooed, "Whatever you say, Locke. You're the boss."

She had a moment of satisfaction, at least, at the
uncertainty that flashed in his usually cool eyes. It
seemed he wasn't quite as impervious to flirtation as
he pretended! If *this* was going to be part of the game,
maybe she didn't need to rewrite the script after all!

"I'd say we're just about halfway there," Josie announced several hours later as they left behind the
last glimpses of rolling hills and moved onto narrow
mountain roads. "Last chance for carsickness pills.
Want one?"

"*Now* you tell me you get carsick?" Locke grinned.
"Some navigator you turned out to be."

Josie twisted in her plush leather seat to catch a
glimpse of Caroline's sleeping face. "I wonder if I
should wake her up and make her take one. Plus"—
she frowned—"I wonder if she remembered to bring
her heart medicine."

"That seat swivels, Josie. You don't have to keep
contorting like a pretzel."

"You've mentioned that fifty times. Say the word
'swivel' one more time and I'm going to clobber
you," she responded sweetly. "I know you think your
gadgets are impressive, but to me they're just more
toys for little boys."

"Here we go again. Your favorite topic, right?"

"You keep giving me ammo, so I keep taking
shots," she teased. "And now that Grandma's asleep,

I don't have to alternate compliments with the insults, so watch out."

"I don't remember any compliments," he countered firmly.

"Are you kidding?" Josie shook her head in feigned disbelief. "I told you what a great driver you are. I gushed about how sweet it is of you to make us so comfortable. I humiliated myself until I could barely stand it, and you didn't even notice?"

"When you said you were going to throw yourself at me, I was expecting physical contact, not common courtesy."

Josie laughed lightly. "Maybe later. Grandma would love to witness a public display of affection. It's been so long since I had a date, she's actually given her blessing to premarital this-and-that. Believe me, for a prude like her, that's quite a switch."

"Premarital this-and-that?" Locke chuckled. "Sounds promising. How long *has* it been?"

"Since I dated? New Year's Eve—I made a resolution, and I've stuck to it."

"That's when you officially stopped dating cops? What about the rest of the male population? You must meet a lot of lawyers, right?"

"Prosecutors mostly. They're just frustrated cops, so they're off limits. I could date my clients, of course, but I'd have to watch my purse and tote a weapon, which takes some of the romance out of it. Then there are the guys in my apartment building—losers. I like them, but they're undatable. Plus I'm on the run all day, and I don't have any support staff except for a half-time secretary, so . . ."

"Sounds like you need a *real* vacation. You're burned out, counselor."

"I know," she sighed. "I've had to scramble just to make ends meet. And now, with Grandma's situation, I may need to find a way to make more money so I can pay her back everything she spent on my schooling." Snuggling back into her seat, she explained, "I wanted to take out school loans, but she insisted on paying. She made it sound like Grandpa left her a huge trust fund that she could never possibly make a dent in by herself. She paid for my brothers' college too. They'll want to pay her back, but both of them just started families and bought houses, so they're in a bind. It's such a mess."

She sifted her fingers through her curls pensively. "At the very least, I'd like to start making her mortgage payments for her so she can keep the house. She's lived there for over forty years, so it must be almost paid off, right?"

Locke shook his head. "She has more than one mortgage, Josie. I doubt she has any equity at all in the place."

"So even if she sold it and moved in with one of us, she'd be penniless? Poor Grandma. She's so proud, Locke—this must be eating her up inside."

"Where do your brothers live?"

"San Diego. And they'd fight over her if they thought they could convince her to move in with one of them. She's great with their babies."

"That's a good plan, then. Right? Even if this reward thing doesn't pan out—"

"I don't want to hear talk like that. This plan is definitely going to work."

Locke's eyes twinkled with amusement. "I know it violates your family code to be honest, but have you considered just sitting down with your brothers and Caroline and working things out?"

"Don't worry about *my* family code. Concentrate on your own. By erasing the blot from your grandfather's record—"

"I never said it was a blot," Locke interrupted sharply. "Don't twist my words, Josie."

"Sorry." She struggled to keep her face expressionless as she pondered this display of temper. She had touched a nerve somehow. It was fascinating, and she wanted to know more.

"I didn't mean to bite your head off," he apologized almost immediately. "Let's talk about something else. Why don't you tell me exactly what made you swear off cops."

Josie smiled slyly. "Are you sure you want to hear this?"

"No, but go ahead anyway."

"Actually, I might be doing you a favor. Once you hear my theory, you may have better luck finding the girl of your dreams. I mean"—she paused dramatically—"you're over thirty and still not married, right? Would you like to know why your relationships always bottom out?"

"This oughta be good."

Josie nodded. "From years of research in the field, I've learned a few things. Guys like you—gunslingers, or wanna-be gunslingers—are initially attracted to strong women. You like the challenge, I think. But in the long run, you don't want an independent, self-sufficient mate. You want someone to protect. A victim who will cling to you and worship the ground you walk on. Choose a helpless little lass next time, Harper, and you'll have better luck in the romance department. I guarantee it."

"What a crock," he murmured.

"I know it's hard to believe, but trust me. I resisted the idea at first too, because I love the world you guys live in. But there's just no room for a strong woman in it. Sometimes it only takes one date, sometimes it takes five or six, but eventually the truth comes out every single time." Squinting slightly at a road sign, she interrupted herself with a quick "This is our turn-off. See the sign? Driftwood Point—seventy miles. Seventy twisty, tortuous miles, and then paradise."

Flipping open the built-in ice chest between their seats, she pulled out a bottle of cola and inclined it toward him. "Thirsty?"

"No thanks."

"Are you hungry? We haven't even touched the sandwiches Grandma made. They're tuna. At least, that's what she says they are."

"Why would she lie about *that?*"

"Tuna is practically all she eats or serves these days," Josie explained. "Now that I know about her finances, I keep remembering those stories about old ladies and cat food—"

"Geez," he groaned. "Where do you get your ideas?"

Her smile widened. Apparently she had touched

another nerve with her talk of strong women. It figured. "So? Are you going to take my advice and find
yourself a damsel in distress?"

Locke eyed her sternly. "First of all, you have no
idea what I want or need in a woman. Second, your
whole theory is based on the assumption that *you're*
a strong woman." Pausing for theatrical effect, he
then insisted, "I actually find that kind of laughable."

A spray of soda from Josie's startled mouth shot
across to the dashboard, coating the tiny screen of
the built-in color TV. While Locke chuckled, she hastily wiped away the droplets, then turned to him and
glared pointedly. "That wasn't funny."

"It wasn't supposed to be. When I said it was laughable, I meant—"

"I know what you meant! You implied that I'm not
a strong woman—"

"I didn't just imply it, I said it straight out." Barely
suppressing a grin, he added, "No offense, right?"

"Go on."

He shrugged. "I'm just saying you're not so tough.
The women I work with—*they're* tough. And I admire
them for it. They're all sharpshooters; most of them
are proficient in martial arts; and every one of them
is highly intelligent. They can handle just about any
situation on their own. On top of all their other quali-
ties, they're stable and rational. Unemotional. To me,
that's a strong woman."

"As opposed to me?"

"Right."

"Because I'm laughable?"

"The concept that you're the self-appointed poster

girl for strength and independence is laughable," he corrected. "As a person, you're obviously great. But strong? I don't think so."

Josie had honestly never been so flabbergasted in her life. "Just because I'm not a sharpshooter—"

"You're sentimental and emotional," he interrupted coolly. "That's not a criticism, by the way. It's actually endearing, but it's not—"

"I'm sentimental where my grandmother is concerned," Josie seethed. "I'm emotional when I hear she's penniless and dying. If your Wonder Women Special Agents wouldn't feel the same way about *their* grandmas, that's not strength. It's bitchy ingratitude."

Locke rolled his eyes as though completely unimpressed by the argument. "Whatever you say."

"I'm strong where it counts! In the courtroom; in a high-security prison interview room; in handling my own finances and relying on my own guts and instincts—" She took a deep breath and muttered, "Never mind. I hardly have to justify myself to you."

"True. *You* attacked *me*, remember? I supposedly represent all the cowpokes and sailors who've broken your heart over the years, right?"

"Be quiet."

"All I'm saying is, maybe you need to reevaluate your theory of the battle of the sexes."

"Let me get this straight. You're saying my relationships have failed because I'm weak and emotional and a lousy shot?"

"I have no idea why your relationships don't work

out. I personally think a guy would be crazy to let you go."

"Because . . . ?"

"Because you're pretty and smart and you make a good living. Plus, you're entertaining. I have no idea why they dumped you—"

"*I* dumped *them!*" she wailed, then caught herself and insisted between gritted teeth, "I'm not discussing this anymore."

"Good."

She fumed in silence for almost a minute, then blurted out, "I can't believe you think I'm weak. *That's* laughable."

"Whatever you say."

"Jackass," she muttered.

"Pardon?"

"I said, if anyone's weak, it was your grandfather. He let Grandma snow him with tears and sobs and fluttering eyelashes when he was supposed to be chasing bad guys."

"I agree."

She had seen his jawline tense, and smiled triumphantly. "That's what this is all about, right? You're here to prove how much tougher you are than him."

"Whatever you say."

"That's why you *have* to believe I'm like Grandma, right? Crying and frightened and desperate for a big strong man to take pity on me. Because," she finished grandly, "if I'm the other kind of woman, this case may not be such a slam dunk for you after all. Right?"

"Sounds like you've got it all figured out," he growled.

"No, not all of it," she corrected softly. "But I've got one thing straight. You're not just an honest man looking for a criminal to bring to justice. You're on some kind of quest here, right?"

"Whatever you say."

He didn't want to talk anymore. His body language told her that and more. The long muscles of his forearms were so tight, she suspected he was mentally strangling the steering wheel in lieu of her neck, and she had to admit that the sight made her proud.

Hitting a nerve with this guy was getting easier and easier, and the self-confidence that he had momentarily stolen from her was now rushing back into place. Content for the moment, she curled up in her seat and pretended to study the map, knowing that the rest of the trip was going to be much longer for Locke Harper than for her.

Driftwood Point was a triumph of nature, from its rugged cliffs to its pounding surf to the twisted cypress and sentrylike redwoods that had somehow managed to thrive despite the sting of salt-laden winds. At the highest point stood the Greybill mansion—a thirty-room brick edifice that would have completely dominated the scene had not the Pacific Ocean stolen the show.

Dotting the landscape were the honeymoon cottages—as humble as the mansion was arrogant. There were eight of them in all, each with one bedroom, one bath, and a kitchenette. No TVs, no phones, no frills.

Josie remained with her grandmother in the gravel parking lot while Locke hiked up to the mansion, which had been converted to a hotel and which also served as the registration desk for all accommodations. Despite the gusty winds, the two women were glad for the chance to climb out of the SUV and stretch their legs after the long, twisty ride.

"Did you and Locke have a fight while I was napping? He's been so gruff since we got here."

"It's like I said, Grandma." Josie shrugged. "The guy is one hundred percent business. I flirted shamelessly with him for almost an hour, and he didn't even notice."

Sweeping her arm out in front of them, she forced her grandmother's attention back to the stupendous view. "Look how those waves pound those rocks. You'd think there'd be nothing left after thousands of years of such abuse."

"Isn't it magnificent? I remember the first time I saw it. So gray and uncontrollable and roaring like a lion! It makes a person feel so insignificant."

Josie wandered close to the edge of the cliff and stared down at a cold stretch of rocky coastline. Although it was the middle of summer, this particular spot had not attracted many beachcombers, despite the profusion of driftwood and tide pools. There was something foreboding about it all, yet Josie could barely wait to get settled into the cottage so they could take the narrow wooden stairway down the steep embankment to the shore.

It was a strange place for a honeymoon, Josie thought. Of course, it was private, so that was a plus.

And supposedly one could spot giant humpback whales passing close to shore on their route between Alaska and Mexico. The effect was breathtaking, but Josie was equally conscious of the chill that dominated the landscape, making her wish she'd brought more sweatshirts and fewer tank tops on the trip.

"Which cottage did you and Grandpa stay in when you were here?"

"That one on the end. Number four." Caroline sighed. "It's the least expensive, because you can't quite view the pretty part of the beach from it. But we didn't mind. It was just nice to be here. Together."

"It's pretty romantic," Josie agreed. "And every view around here is a great one. It looks like the mansion is the only really good spot for actually looking out to sea though. It's great that they've converted that to rooms too, don't you think?"

Caroline grimaced at the thought. "It's haunted, you know. That man was murdered right there in the study. Right beyond those huge French doors that open onto the veranda."

"And that's where you were standing when it happened? I mean, on that veranda?"

"Yes. I was trying to get my bearings after a dizzy spell on the dance floor. I wandered away from your grandfather and got a bit turned around. The guests were mostly on the wide veranda that faces the ocean. We weren't supposed to be in the private areas."

"Are you remembering any details that could help Locke?"

Caroline frowned. "Sometimes it's hard to separate

imagination from true memory, especially at my age. Maybe after I rest a bit, I'll be more helpful."

"You want to rest again so soon?" Josie slipped her arm around the frail shoulders. "Are you feeling up to all this?"

"I feel fine, Josie. Just a little weary."

"When was the last time you saw a doctor?"

Caroline stared at her in surprise. "Do I look that bad? Really, Josie, you can't expect me to have the energy of a twenty-seven-year-old." A soft smile lit her lips. "I can tell you're dying to go to the beach. As soon as Locke gets back, take him down there. Maybe he'll put his arm around you, to protect you from the breezes."

Josie tried not to grin at the thought. Even though Locke's mood had softened a little toward the end of the drive, he was undoubtedly in no mood to cuddle. It would be fun to "throw" herself at him, knowing it would annoy him at the same time it pleased Caroline. "Here he comes."

"He looks a little more relaxed," Caroline observed, staring intently toward the lone figure as he crunched his way back across the parking lot. "I imagine it's hard for a man like that to really be on vacation."

"He's *not* on vacation. He's on a case. Remember what I told you about his grandfather last night?"

"Yes. I think it's sweet."

"Well, maybe not as sweet as it sounded at first. I think there's more going on with that than we know, so take your cue from me, okay? If his questions start turning strange, we'll need to rethink this little get-away. Remember, I'm here as your lawyer."

"You sound as though you've soured on him," Caroline complained. "Do you still find him attractive?"

"More than ever." Josie grinned. "He's got a dangerous side now, and you know how sexy that can be."

"Well, then, start letting him know how you feel. You can't be subtle with a man like Locke."

"Probably not. Let's see if the direct approach works." With a wink toward her grandmother, Josie turned and sprinted the distance between herself and their escort, then threw her arms around his neck and whispered, "Play along, please. Grandma made me do this."

Locke chuckled despite himself. "Finally, the good stuff begins." Running his hands over her arms, he observed, "You've got goose bumps. I hope you brought a sweater or something."

"You're supposed to put your arm around me and keep me warm."

He complied willingly, then walked her back toward Caroline and the SUV. "Seriously, Josie, I didn't realize it'd be so cold here in the middle of summer. But they told me they weatherproofed the cottages lately, so they shouldn't be too drafty. And there's supposedly a huge fireplace in the rec room up at the big house. We can use those facilities whenever we want."

"Grandma thinks it's haunted, so I don't think we'll be spending much time there."

Locke chuckled again. "Haunted? Because of the murder? You and Caroline really do like to drag every possible ounce of drama out of a situation, don't you?"

"Speaking of which: It's showtime, so start playing hard to get." After a few more steps in Caroline's direction, she turned toward Locke, stroked his cheek with her finger, and murmured, "Thanks for checking us in and everything. It's so nice to have a man around to take care of us."

Pulling away, he eyed her sternly and insisted, "Hop back into the car now, and we'll park up behind the cottage. We should get all this stuff unpacked while the weather's still clear."

"And then you and Josie should go for a walk on the beach," Caroline added helpfully.

"Aren't you coming?"

"I can't handle those stairs anymore," Caroline explained. "They're too steep and rickety. I'll just fix myself a cup of tea and watch from the cottage."

"I can help you down the steps, Caroline. Josie and I don't want to go to the beach alone. What's the point of that?"

Josie hid a smile as Locke's performance frustrated the determined matchmaker. "Well, if you don't see the point in strolling on a beach with a beautiful woman," Caroline murmured, "I don't suppose there's anything left to say."

"I'm here to interview *you*, not your granddaughter," Locke reminded her. "Let's just settle in for now, shall we? We can call up to the big house and order room service. Maybe once you've eaten, you'll be ready to talk about the night of the robbery."

"We'll see," Caroline sighed as she climbed back into her seat.

After Locke had shut the rear door, Josie whispered, "That was great. If I didn't know better, I'd think this trip was all business for you instead of a personal vendetta."

"Don't start with me again," he warned good-naturedly. "I'll play along for a while, but I have my limits. Get her to talk to me, Josie, or I may have to change my strategy and tell her about the reward."

Josie frowned ominously. "You're making it tough for me to pretend to be lovestruck."

"Sorry. How's this?" With a wicked grin he pulled her flush against his chest. "Shall we put on a show for Grandma?"

She loved the rush of heat, after the combined chill of the wind and his bad mood, and her goose bumps disappeared instantly, replaced by a tingle that shot straight to her toes. To her delight, Locke's body was responding just as easily, and she dared for just a moment to enjoy that too before teasing, "You're taking the expression 'hard to get' a little too literally."

"I notice you're not pulling away."

"It's cold out." She pouted playfully. "In weather like this, a guy with a big gun comes in handy."

He chuckled proudly. "I hope Caroline can't read lips. She'd have to wash your mouth out." Pressing his hand against the small of her back, he coaxed her to grind against him a bit. "So? We'll unpack and take that walk on the beach, right?"

"What about room service?" she reminded him breathlessly. "Aren't you hungry?"

"Ravenous." His free hand moved to cup her chin toward his face. "By the way, we've had a slight change of plans. I'm going to pretend to be love-struck too."

His mouth descended to hers, tasting her with gentle pressure, and then she gasped in delight as his tongue began to probe. Never in a million years had she expected him to behave this way, especially in front of Grandma! At this rate, he would be out of control in seconds, but she had no desire to slow him down. The tingling feeling was deepening, concentrating itself into waves of delicious expectation that made her want to wrap her legs around him right there in the parking lot!

Then he stopped, as easily as he'd begun, and grinned down at her with malevolent glee. "Strong and independent, my ass. You're probably the weakest woman I've ever met. But, baby"—his steely eyes twinkled wildly—"you sure can kiss."

FOUR

Locke knew he should feel guilty but, standing on the beach within inches of the pounding surf he was instead supremely self-satisfied if not altogether smug. That kiss—that deep, dangerous, powerful kiss—had taught Joselyn Galloway a long-overdue lesson, and he'd be darned if he was going to apologize for it! Remember it? Yeah, probably to his dying day. Apologize for it? Never.

She had brought it on herself, hadn't she? The whole trip from Sutterville to the coast had been one long battle of wits. A battle of Josie's making. Someone had been bound to win. Which meant someone had been bound to lose. Why should he feel guilty over *that*? Maybe she wouldn't be so quick to challenge an unknown opponent the next time she was feeling "strong and independent." He had probably done her a favor!

Locke had been in the driver's seat during the trip, but it had felt more like a hot seat. Or worse, like he'd been on a witness stand, being grilled by a prosecutor. It seemed funny now—in fact, he'd love to see

Josie in action someday in an actual courtroom—but at the time it had been annoying and frustrating. It was as though her brain never rested, never missed an opportunity to explore and exploit an opponent's weaknesses. And she had those eyes and that body for backup, just in case some man dared attempt to use actual logic on her. Never in his life had he met a woman like her, and there had been a moment or two when he'd actually thought she might be able to gain the upper hand for good.

Now, because of one perfectly engineered kiss, Special Agent Locke Harper was back in the driver's seat. He intended to stay there.

"I'm telling you, Grandma, he's the ultimate jack-ass! Just because he's marginally attractive, he honestly believes he's God's gift! He caught me off guard, and so to that extent it was *my* fault, but that doesn't change the fact that the guy's a menace. If the FBI knew he was manhandling women in public parking lots, his career would be over. Right?

"I mean, let's face it. He's nice-looking. I'd be lying if I said he wasn't." Josie nodded vigorously as she paced the small sitting area that adjoined the kitchen in Cottage No. 4. "It makes sense that he's had some success in the kissing field. And I'm a little rusty. So he caught me off guard and proceeded to take advantage of the situation. He's lucky I didn't slap his arrogant face. Right?"

She felt like screeching in frustration, remembering the tone he'd dared to take with her. As though they'd been at war and he'd vanquished her, or something ridiculous like that. And, of course, he hadn't played fair. He had manipulated the fact that her grandmother was watching and they were supposed to be pretending to have chemistry, "pretending" being the operative word.

Not that it hadn't felt good in a generic sort of way. Josie had *allowed* it to feel good for the sake of her poor, weak-hearted grandma. If Locke Harper was conceited enough to take that as some sort of tribute to his masculinity, fine. But to imply that it was a sign of weakness on Josie's part was preposterous.

"He's got problems, Grandma. Serious problems. Want to hear my theory? He's been handed everything on a silver platter just because he's good-looking and smart. No one has ever taken the time to actually challenge him, and so, of course, when he meets a strong woman, he feels threatened. And so he uses the weapon that usually works for him. Sex appeal. Right?"

She spun to seek approval in her grandmother's eyes, then blanched when she saw tears instead. "What's wrong? Oh, no, don't tell me you really thought Locke and I would live happily ever after. Oh, Grandma . . ."

"It's nothing like that," Caroline assured her unhappily. "It's just . . . well, all this!" Her hand swept about herself to encompass not only the cozy cottage but also the seascape that was visible through half-open French doors adjoining a small redwood deck. "There are so many memories here. I had no idea it would be so unsettling."

Mortified that she had once again been oblivious to her grandmother's plight, Josie strode across the room, plopped onto the tweed couch, and threw her arms around the older woman's neck. "Here I am, going on and on about that meaningless kiss! I'm so sorry, sweetie. Tell me what's bothering you." She adopted a coaxing tone. "Are you remembering the murder and the investigation? Or Grandpa and the honeymoon? Tell me what's wrong."

"I miss him so terribly," Caroline admitted. "I fell in love with him here, you know."

"You did? I thought you were childhood sweethearts."

"Oh, we were," she assured her granddaughter wistfully. "But here, in this place—" Caroline hesitated, then admitted, "I saw a side of him here that took my breath away."

Josie nodded again. "Because you two made love here for the first time?"

Caroline flushed. "There was that, of course. But it was much, much more. It's almost like . . ." She hesitated again, as though unsure of whether Josie could possibly understand. "Your grandfather wasn't much of a talker—do you remember?"

"The strong, silent type," Josie agreed. "Just like Dad."

"Exactly. But here he and I would walk on the beach and talk for hours. About our dreams. Our fears. Our goals. I learned more about him that week that I'd learned in all the years I'd known him."

"Wow."

"And then that awful Greybill man was murdered,

and it was as though all the warmth and safety went right out of our lives."

"I see what you mean. Paradise one minute, brutal reality the next. And of course"—Josie frowned—"you couldn't just leave. Because of the damned FBI. They're a menace, just like I said."

"They wouldn't let any of us leave. At least, not until they'd searched our cottage and our cars and our luggage. It was so humiliating, especially for your grandfather, because he was such a private man by nature. And then, because I was the only witness, they kept focusing on me, when all I wanted to do was go home."

"How terrible." Josie hugged her grandmother close in a vain attempt to soften the memory. "I wish I'd been there. I would have made Locke's grandfather back off."

"Your grandfather did his best, but there was only so much he could do. Still"—her green eyes sparkled—"he was my hero. I hope he knew that."

"Good grief," Josie moaned. "It's so romantic! Don't you see? It's like they always say. Anything that doesn't kill you makes you stronger. I guess that's true for love too. The experience you and Grandpa had here made your love super strong."

Caroline shook her head. "It tested us, but we would have been happier if it had never happened. If only I hadn't been stupid enough to wander into that awful Greybill man's study."

"You keep calling him that. Was he awful to you personally or just generally awful?"

"Personally?" Caroline's laugh was uncharacteristically bitter. "None of us were persons to him, Josie. He saw us as pests—the people in the cottages. That's what he called us. Everyone knew what a snob he was. We were warned not to go near his precious mansion or to step foot on the part of the beach that was directly in front of it, for fear we might spoil his view."

"What a creep. So why were you and Grandpa at the Fourth of July party up there?"

Caroline's green eyes seethed with resentment. "He didn't want the honeymooners having our own celebrations down here. No fireworks or bonfires were allowed. If we wished to celebrate, we could attend the party but were given strict instructions on how to act. So we wouldn't interfere with the real guests' holiday."

Josie dug her fingernails into her palms, desperate to control her protective instincts. After all, it'd been almost fifty years, and that awful Greybill man was dead. All Grandma really needed now was closure.

"So, you went to the party. And you got dizzy. And so you wandered into Mr. Greybill's study. Right?"

"I was looking for a cool rag for my forehead. Instead, I found Henry Greybill himself."

"Was he rude to you?"

Caroline bit her lip. "I suppose he tried, in his own way, to be civil. He told me to sit on the veranda and he'd fetch a cold washcloth and some brandy."

Josie studied her quizzically. "That was decent of him."

"I suppose you had to be there." Caroline sniffed. "He would never have treated his society guests the way he treated me."

"Okay. Tell me what happened next."

"I still felt woozy, and he took so long, I was debating whether to just go back and find your grandfather. Then I heard noises."

"What kind of noises?"

Caroline threw up her hands in frustration. "That's what the detective kept asking! I was dizzy, Josie. I was barely able to keep my footing, much less analyze the situation. All I knew was, something was wrong."

"Okay, okay. You heard noises, and you knew something was wrong, and so you went into the awful man's study. That was brave, Grandma."

"No, it was stupid."

Josie winced. That was the second time her grandmother had used the word "stupid"—a word that usually was not allowed in the Galloway family. It seemed impossible that a person could be this upset over something that had happened half a century earlier, but Josie wasn't about to give up. "You went into his study, and then what?"

"And he was lying on the ground. A bottle of brandy was spilled next to him. I suppose I thought he'd had a heart attack, and so I leaned down, and he was so lifeless. I just knew . . ."

"And then?"

"And then I ran out, back onto the veranda, and I don't know if I shouted or just . . . well, just whimpered, but a waiter saw me or heard me and came and then . . . well, pandemonium struck, of course. It seemed like an eternity before I was safely in your grandfather's arms. Then the police came. *That* was a nightmare. Then later it was the FBI. Because Grey-bill was a candidate for Congress, you know."

"Locke mentioned that. He said there were a lot of important politicians at that party."

"They were treated with kid gloves. We, of course, weren't. But Locke's grandfather was a gentleman through and through. I suppose that's where Locke gets his manners."

Josie grimaced.

"You're still angry with him for kissing you? I have to admit, Josie—" Caroline paused as though about to enter delicate territory. "I'm a little confused about that. I thought you *wanted* him to kiss you. Didn't you say you flirted with him in the car while I was sleeping?"

"I wanted him to *kiss* me, not *maul* me. Weren't you watching? It was a disgusting spectacle."

"You didn't seem to mind," Caroline chided. "I think you gave him the wrong impression. You can't very well flirt with a young man, and hang on him, and tease, and then be offended when he—"

"Grandma?"

"Yes?"

"Maybe we should drop it. Let's get back to the story of the robbery."

"I'm just saying Locke's a gentleman. He'd never do anything unless he thought you were willing. He's just not that kind of man."

"He's perfect," Josie drawled. "End of discussion."

"You really should go and make up with him, Josie. A week is too short to spend any time quarreling."

Too short? On the contrary, a week with Locke Harper sounded like an eternity to Josie. She had no intention of spending one more minute with him than was absolutely necessary to get her grandmother the reward money. In fact, she was hoping to bypass the agent's involvement completely from here on out and simply solve the robbery herself.

"I have a better idea, Grandma. Why don't you and I go up to the mansion and do a little investigating? Maybe you'll remember something, and you can surprise Locke over dinner with the news."

"I'm tired, Josie. I'd like to nap before dinner."

"Sure. You nap, and I'll read. We'll go up to the veranda after dinner."

"I'm afraid that's out of the question. I couldn't bear to go up to that dreadful place. Not ever again. You and Locke will have to go alone."

Josie felt a mild but definite stab of panic at the finality of the statement. "You told Locke you wanted to return to the scene of the crime, Grandma. That's why he brought us here, remember?"

"This is close enough," Caroline insisted. "I never said I'd go into the mansion itself. Anyway, I don't believe that's the reason Locke brought us here. I think he's completely smitten with you."

"He brought us here to solve a crime, in honor of his grandfather. Plus, he's trying to prove he can stay focused on a case better than his grandfather could. It's complicated, Grandma, but believe me, it's not about romance."

"How do you explain the kiss, then?" Caroline smiled. "You said yourself he was practically devouring you."

"Mauling me," Josie reminded her weakly. "Anyway, you have to take my word for it. He's going to be very annoyed when he hears you won't go up to the mansion. He's going to bring up hypnosis again, and that's worse, right?" She patted her grandmother's hand. "Locke and I will be with you every step of the way. We won't let anything bad happen. Just spend five minutes on that veranda—"

"I don't want to discuss it anymore, Joselyn. I can't possibly go up to that awful place, and even if I could, there's no need for it. I can remember just as well from here. And once I'm rested, I plan to start going over the entire episode in my head, over and over and over, until I have a wonderful clue for Locke."

"Okay, okay. Just rest, then. I'll explain it to him somehow." *So much for giving him the silent treatment,* she added glumly to herself as she reached for a soft, navy-blue hooded sweatshirt.

She knew he was down on the beach somewhere, laughing at her and savoring his "victory." She wanted to wipe the smirk from his face, but payback would have to wait a while. For the time being, at least, she needed to grit her teeth and be charming, or the reward money would be history. What a burn!

"Locke?"

He turned, half expecting to feel the sting of her palm across his jaw, but instead her expression was almost docile. It didn't make sense. "Hi, Josie."

"Hi." She flushed and added lamely, "Can we have a truce? I need to talk to you about Grandma."

He felt an unexpected wave of protectiveness toward Caroline Galloway. "Is she feeling okay? Was the ride too much for her?"

"She's confused. Haunted by too many memories, I guess. The murder, and Grandpa, and all that. I'm worried this trip might be bad for her heart."

"Do you want me to take the two of you home? We could probably make it by midnight—"

"No, no." Josie smiled gratefully. "I need to get that fifty thousand dollars for her. But we have to be very understanding and very sensitive. I don't want to pressure her about anything."

"No one's going to pressure Caroline," he promised. "We'll have a nice, relaxing dinner, and tomorrow morning we'll head up to the mansion. Maybe something'll click in her memory and we can get this over with. But if nothing comes to her, that's fine too. It's no big deal either way."

"I'm kind of glad to hear you say that, because . . ." Josie took a deep breath, then her smile grew a bit too bright and cheery. "You're going to laugh when you hear this."

Locke knew from that expression that there had been a new development—something big—that Josie feared might threaten her grandmother's chances of claiming the reward money. It explained why she hadn't given him either a cold shoulder or a tongue lashing over the kiss. She was on the defensive, and he couldn't help but enjoy it. "I could use a laugh. What's up?"

"Well, actually, it's more ironic than actually funny.

It turns out Grandma's a little bit afraid to go up to the mansion."

"That's understandable, Josie. Like I said, we can wait until tomorrow. There's no rush, is there?"

"Actually, she'd rather not go up there at all."

"Pardon?"

"She says it's out of the question." Josie's smile faded. "It's sad, don't you think? She's obviously much more traumatized by the experience than any of us realized."

"Let me guess: She never had any intention of going up there. Why doesn't that surprise me?" Locke grumbled. "All that scene-of-the-crime crap was a con job. It's vintage Galloway. Why tell the truth when a lie is so much more effective?"

"I didn't know she was lying, Locke. Honest. And I don't blame you for being annoyed. But I can't bear to give her a hard time about it. After all—"

After all, she has a bad heart." He shook his head in amused annoyance. "Like I said, the whole thing's priceless. She's doing the same thing today she did fifty years ago."

"Excuse me?"

"She was fragile then too. For different reasons, but still, it was basically the same routine. I don't know why I bothered. In fact"—he straightened and suggested briskly—"let's just drop it altogether."

"No! She needs the money. Please, Locke—"

"I meant let's just drop the charade. *All* the charades, in fact. You and Caroline can sit back and enjoy a week at the beach. I'll just do what I would have done if I'd come alone as *originally planned.*" Clearing his throat, he added more gently, "If I figure out where the jewels are, great. Caroline can have the reward. If not, at least she'll have gotten some rest."

"That's so sweet of you." Josie sighed with exaggerated relief. "I'm sorry I called you a jackass."

He grinned reluctantly. "Since we're apologizing, I'm sorry about that crack I made after I kissed you. It was a cheap shot."

Josie shrugged. "You completely misunderstood that, you know. I was *pretending* to be swept off my feet—for Grandma's sake. Apparently, I'm a better actress than I knew. Sorry if I gave you the wrong impression."

"Yeah, right. It was all a misunderstanding." He chuckled as he added, "You're too much, Josie."

"Whatever. So . . ." She paused to scan the beach longingly. "I know we should get right to work, but it's so gorgeous here. How about a compromise? We explore the beach until dinner. After that, Grandma can go to bed early, and you and I can start reviewing the files."

"Pardon?"

"You brought the files, didn't you? I saw the old briefcase you had in the back of the car. Wasn't it your grandpa's?"

He nodded warily.

"Like I said, you're sweet. And very sentimental for a jackass." Her smile was almost dazzling. "I think we'll make a wonderful team now that we've got the ground rules out of the way."

"Josie?"

"Yes?"

"Maybe I didn't make myself clear. You're off the hook. Explore to your heart's content. Collect shells, write your memoirs—whatever you want. You're on vacation. I'll handle the investigation on my own."

"Don't be silly. I can help. In some ways you're too close to this, you know. I can bring objectivity—"

"No thanks."

She placed her hands on her hips and chided, "Don't be so stubborn. Two heads—"

"No, thank you. Case closed."

Her emerald eyes narrowed. "Are you afraid to work with me?"

"Huh?"

"I'm obviously a threat to your manhood. Maybe it's because of the way your grandpa bungled the case. I'm sorry about that, but we don't really have a choice. If I don't help, and we don't convince Grandma that she played a part in solving the case, she'll never accept the reward money."

Locke's temples were beginning to pound. "You're doing it again."

"Doing what?"

"Making things complicated." He rubbed his eyes, then insisted, "I *need* to work alone. I can see now that it's the only way I'll be able to concentrate. If you want to tell Caroline you helped me, no problem. Lie to your heart's content. Just leave me out of it from now on."

Josie seemed about to argue with him, then she sighed in apparent defeat. "I need to *pretend* to help you, at least. Don't sabotage that, okay? Play along— just for a few days."

"Fine."

"And I need to pretend we're romantically involved. Is that going to be a problem?"

"Back to that?" He was honestly amazed. "I thought you'd had enough of that after the—"

"My grandmother adores the idea that you and I are an item," Josie interrupted briskly. "She's thrilled to think one of her matchmaking schemes finally panned out, and if I can bring a little joy into the poor, sick woman's—"

"Fine! Pretend to help me, pretend to date me, pretend I'm your long-lost brother if it makes you happy. Just don't ask *me* to lie. Understood?"

"I suppose." Her eyes sparkled mischievously. "You're such a boy scout sometimes. I'll bet those big, strong, sharpshooting Amazons at the Bureau love that about you. Right?"

Her confidence was returning, he noted sourly. Any minute now she'd become downright obnoxious if he didn't do something to remind her that two could play that game. Fortunately, he had the perfect threat. "Don't make me teach you a lesson again, Ms. Galloway. Not that I didn't enjoy it the first time, but I thought we declared a truce."

"You're referring to the kiss again?" Josie smiled. "You just can't get it out of your mind, can you? That's pathetic, Harper. Sounds like maybe you should get an actual life instead of imagining conquests and reliving your grandpa's old cases."

Even as his eyes narrowed, he had to give her credit. She had taken his best shot and rendered it harmless. From now on, if he dared refer to how he'd gotten the upper hand with that kiss, it would be characterized as proof that he was somehow hung up on it—and her. It was brilliant!

And it also wasn't over. To his amazement, she stepped close and slipped her hands along his shoulders until they came to rest on the back of his neck. "No hard feelings, right? You'll find someone someday, Locke. I'm sure of it. You're too honest and successful to stay single forever."

"Yeah? Thanks for letting me down easy," he drawled. "Like I said, you're too much."

He liked the way the big green eyes bubbled with merriment, even if it was at his expense. Then she brushed her lips across his, and it was all he could do to keep his own hands at his sides. His body was remembering the kiss. In fact, it was remembering the dancing from the night before too. And all the arguing during the drive that now seemed more like foreplay than anything else.

And suddenly, he knew exactly what was happening. His body was in imminent danger of being lovestruck. It was a classic case of history trying to repeat itself. Fortunately, Locke's mind was still clear—in fact, it was clearer than ever. Because now he knew exactly how his grandfather had been seduced into blowing the case. And from that knowledge, he also knew how to avoid the same fate.

The Galloway women had what it took to drive a man crazy, and they knew how to use it to manipulate distasteful situations. His grandfather hadn't had advance warning, and so he had fallen easily for the feigned vulnerability and distracting sentimentality.

But Locke had been introduced to the twisted brilliance that lay behind Josie's seductive eyes, pouty lips, and responsive body. So he could resist, do his job, and find the jewels. "Now, if Grandma asks if we kissed and made up," Josie was explaining, "you can tell her yes without lying. Right?"

"Yeah. Thanks for being so thoughtful."

"My pleasure." She stepped away and scanned the beach once more. "Where should we start? With those cliffs over there?"

"You tell me."

"Really?" She beamed with delight. "Okay, I say the cliffs. There must be a thousand crevices in those rocks, and probably dozens are big enough to hide stolen jewels in. We'll have to consider every one."

"Whatever you say."

"I'm not saying your grandfather didn't check them all thoroughly when he was here. I'm sure he did. Right?"

"According to his notes, yes, he did."

"But it wouldn't hurt to check again, right?"

"Whatever you say."

"I like you like this," Josie admitted. "What exactly brought you into line?"

"Exhaustion," he admitted in return. "And a sense that resistance, as they say, would be futile."

FIVE

Locke insisted that the honeymoon resort should have been named *Drab*wood Point, due to the unending lengths of gray water, gray sand, gray wood, and gray weather, but Josie staunchly defended both the name and the place itself. In less than an hour she managed to amass a huge collection of driftwood sculptures, carved lovingly by the angry sea from the wreckage of ships. A dolphin, a spearhead—even one shaped just like a toy gun. She tried to sneak up on Locke with that one, but he proved to be annoyingly well trained, flipping her easily onto her back without taking even a momentary break from his search of the rocky crevices.

Still, if Josie had named the resort, she would have called it after the giant natural archway that had been worn, by time, tide, and wind through a rocky cliff just out of sight of the cottages. It was like the ruins of a huge bridge leading to nowhere, and the young defense attorney fantasized about the giants who had built it, and traveled it, in search of adventure before it crumbled into the ocean centuries before the first humans arrived in North America. The bridge could have stretched, in days gone by, all the way to Hawaii. And, she told herself playfully, Locke Harper would have used it in a heartbeat to find white sands and balmy weather in place of this rugged landscape. What a wimp!

Even Josie had her limits, however, and when the gusts of winds began to actually pelt her with rough sand, she sought out her companion and complained. "Five more minutes and I won't have any features left on my face."

He nodded grimly. "Let's get out of here. I'm hungry anyway." Arm in arm, they battled the stinging air together as they headed for the steps that would take them to cover. "When they said this was a beach resort, I expected paradise, not Son of Twister."

"Grandma says it'll be beautiful when the sun comes out."

"*If* the sun comes out."

Josie nodded, then approached the weathered staircase warily. "It's a good thing Grandma's not going to use these. They should be condemned."

"The whole place should—" Locke stopped and grinned self-consciously. "I don't usually complain so much. You're a bad influence, Galloway."

Josie stuck out her tongue, then rushed up the steps to avoid repercussions. Fortunately the steep, rough structure, while seemingly precarious, was actually quite well built, and she made it to the top without incident. Then Locke had his arm around her shoulders again in a companionlike, nonthreatening way,

and they ambled to the cottage as though they'd been
friends this way for years.

Josie had expected her grandmother to be resting.
Still, she wasn't surprised to find instead that a feast
had been laid out on the tiny redwood deck on their
behalf. It was predictably romantic. Candles waiting
to be lit, champagne waiting to be sipped, music waft-
ing toward them from the dance floor of the mansion.

"Room service," Caroline informed them brightly.
"I hope you like clams, Locke."

"Love 'em."

The older woman beamed at the couple. "I'm glad
to see you two are getting along a little better."

"Locke got down on one knee and begged my for-
giveness," Josie explained. "So I gave him a break."

"That was sweet of you, Locke."

Josie sent her escort a playful smirk. "He told me
he never met a woman as strong and independent as
me—"

"That's enough." Locke laughed.

"I agree with Locke completely." Caroline's smile
was angelic. Turning to the agent, she added, "You
can tell me your version of the so-called apology while
Josie changes into her red dress for dinner."

Josie shook her head. "I'll wash up, and that's it.
We're eating casual, right? When you're ready to dine
up at the fancy mansion"—she paused to arch a mischievous eyebrow—"I'll consider getting all dolled
up."

"I for one definitely need to shower," Locke admitted. "That beach was a hellhole—pardon my language, Caroline."

"It's not at its best today, Locke. But wait until the sun comes out. You'll be amazed."

"I'm sure I will. Josie? Did you want to use the bathroom first?"

"Help yourself. I'm just going to change into a fresh T-shirt and kick back. Grandma, I hope that's a pitcher of margaritas."

"It's lemonade, but there's champagne for you. The resort gave it to us as a welcoming gift. And, of course, I remembered to order a beer for Locke."

"Thanks, Caroline. You're the best." He kissed her cheek, then hefted his suitcase onto the couch and began to rummage for a clean shirt. "By the way, I'll be fine out here on the sofa. You two ladies should take the bedroom."

Caroline nodded. "Josie said you insisted on that during the ride up, so I already unpacked my things. It seems unfair though. You're paying for this whole trip, and you don't even get a decent bed!"

"The FBI's paying for the trip," Josie lied firmly. "So I hope you charged this dinner, Grandma."

The older woman flushed. "They made me charge it. But *I* insist on paying Locke back once we get home. The dinner, at least, will be my treat."

Locke grimaced. "It's like Josie said. The Bureau's picking up the tab, so charge whatever you like. If we find the jewels, it'll be well worth it. And if not, it's still the government's treat. No arguments."

Josie sent him a grateful glance. Apparently, even boy scouts could lie sometimes! She was almost tempted to wear the red tube dress, just to thank him, but resisted the urge and headed for the bedroom to find a modest pink T-shirt in which to dine.

Caroline was loving the role of hostess and, to Locke's credit, he was performing admirably in the role of honored guest. Which, of course, made Josie practically invisible, but she didn't really mind. It was wonderful to see her grandmother so happy, even if Caroline *did* seem to laugh too indulgently at the agent's jokes while practically ignoring Josie's clever retorts. Such, the granddaughter decided, were the ways of the matchmaker. Who was she to question them?

"So, Locke," Caroline was insisting sweetly. "Tell us all about your cases. Working for the FBI must be so exciting. And such a responsibility! It gives me goose bumps."

"It has its moments."

"What are you working on now? I mean, besides this silly Greybill case. There must be something more important that you're spending your time on."

"Actually," he admitted carefully, "my partner and I are investigating a serial arsonist. It's one of the most difficult cases I've ever been involved with."

"A serial arsonist," Caroline marveled. "And are you developing a profile of this person?"

Locke grinned. "You know your stuff, don't you?"

"I watch a lot of TV," Caroline confirmed. "And I read incessantly. Josie can tell you that."

Josie nodded. "Grandma's really into mystery and

suspense. But usually it's serial *killers*. A profile for a serial *arsonist* sounds fascinating. Let me guess." She sent Caroline a conspiratorial smile. "I'll bet he used to set his cornflakes on fire as a child."

When no one responded, Josie added lamely, "Get it? A 'cereal' arsonist? He set his *cornflakes* on fire?" She tapped her fork as though it were a microphone. "Is this thing *on*?"

"Very clever, dear," Caroline soothed. "Cornflakes, cereal, serial arsonist. It's a lovely joke."

A "lovely" joke? Josie glared toward Locke, who was grinning broadly and who now dared to say, "It was funny, Josie. Don't feel bad."

"I don't—" She gritted her teeth. "Tell us about the arsonist, Agent Harper. We're breathless with anticipation."

He grew visibly more guarded. "There's not much to tell. And I don't usually talk about active cases. Especially when I'm with two such beautiful companions."

Josie sent him a pointed what-a-jackass scowl, then asked Caroline, "Wouldn't you rather talk about the Greybill case? That's why we're here, after all. I'm sure Locke the Magnificent has some wonderful ideas about how to solve the robbery."

"Actually, I do." Locke's attention was focused squarely on Caroline. "Josie told me you don't want to go up to the mansion."

"Are you angry with me?"

"Never. But I do have a suggestion." His smile was sinfully warm. "Do you hear the music? It's coming from a brand-new redwood deck they built off the main dining room last year. I took a look at it while I was checking us in. It's great, and—" He paused for emphasis. "It doesn't hold any memories for you, right? I mean, it wasn't even here when the crime was committed."

"There were no redwood decks at Driftwood Point back then. Not out here in the cottages and not up there."

"So, let's go up there tomorrow night. Not to solve the case—that's something that will either happen or won't. Let's go up there so that you can see the truth, which is that there's nothing to be afraid of. We can have a great dinner, maybe even dance a little, and you can see the mansion for what it is. Just a house. No ghosts, no dangers. Just a place to relax and enjoy yourself."

Caroline's green eyes were filling with tears. "I want to remember, Locke. I meant it when I said I wanted to help."

"That's the point," he soothed. "I don't really care if you remember or not. What matters is that you leave this mess behind you, once and for all, when you leave this place. I think my grandfather would have wanted that for you, Caroline. If I can't solve the case, maybe I can at least give him that."

Josie's own emerald eyes were beginning to sting, even though she suspected Agent Harper was just telling them what they wanted to hear. Either way, it was doing wonders for Caroline, who seemed to relax completely for the first time since their arrival.

"I'm so glad we let you talk us into coming here, Locke," the older woman gushed. "I'll think about what you said. Maybe I *should* go up to that awful place, just once. To banish the ghosts, like you said. We'll have to see about that. And in the meantime"— she dimpled prettily—"why don't you ask my granddaughter to dance? You know you want to."

"Dance here?" Josie protested uneasily, glancing down at her faded jeans and clean but hopelessly casual T-shirt. "I can barely hear the music."

"They're playing 'A Fine Romance,' " Locke informed her quietly. "But if you don't feel comfortable . . ." He stood and bowed toward Caroline. "Mrs. Galloway? Would you do me the honor?"

It was hokey and completely transparent, but still, when Josie saw the spark of delight in her grandmother's eyes, she couldn't help but adore Special Agent Locke Harper. He had a way of being firm with Caroline, yet fully respecting her limits, that Josie would have loved to master. Maybe she could learn a thing or two from him this week.

But if she really wanted to learn something, she knew where she needed to look—in that antique briefcase, which Locke had naively left lying right in plain sight of the dining table, although conveniently out of sight of the two dancers. It was as though he were almost begging Josie to invade his privacy! And since he had made it clear on the beach that he didn't plan on sharing his files with her, she really had no choice but to slip out of her seat, grab the case, and pull it farther into the shadows of the living room, where she was relieved to discover that the latch, while solid, was not locked.

There was no time to admire the buttery texture

of the leather, but Josie knew instinctively that conditioning this case, and keeping it in such wonderful shape, was another tribute paid by a loving grandson to his childhood hero. It was so sweet! And he had reorganized the files too. That was evident from the newness of the two accordion folders that held equal parts of the case's contents.

A quick peek told Josie that the papers in one folder were considerably older than those in the other. The old ones were probably originals, she guessed, while the newer ones might be recent photocopies of FBI files, made by Locke in preparation for the trip. Although she was dying to pore over the handwritten journals and notes, it seemed slightly less invasive to tackle the photocopies first, and so she tucked that folder under her arm, fastened the clasp carefully, and placed the case back on the floor beside the couch. Then she scurried into the bedroom and stuck the contraband under the queen-size bed she'd be sharing later with Caroline.

By the time she got back to the table, the dancers had returned to their seats and were conversing lightly, as though they hadn't missed Josie at all. *The perfect crime,* she congratulated herself. "I was just in the bedroom, putting cream on my cheeks. They got a little burned, which I guess proves the sun was up there someplace today, even though we didn't see it."

"The worst burns happen on overcast days," Caroline warned. "You should bring lotion down to the beach with you religiously and have Locke put it on your back and shoulders."

Josie turned to Locke and sighed, "My grandma, the pimp."

"Joselyn Galloway! Behave yourself."

"Make up your mind, Grandma. I can behave, or I can let Locke rub lotion all over me."

"Or we could dance," Locke suggested evenly. "It's nice out on the deck, Josie. You can hear the music better out there."

Josie winced, wondering how he intended to play this part of the charade. Was he back to pretending to resist? Was he going to try to maul her again under the mistaken impression that she'd allow it for Caroline's sake? Or did he just like to dance? He certainly knew the names of all the old songs, didn't he? And this was his vacation, in a sense, so maybe he was just trying to enjoy himself a little.

Still, it was disconcerting this time, when he took her into his arms. She was remembering the way their kiss had rocked her body and robbed her of her wits. His hand on the small of her back seemed too close to other, more dangerous areas. The hardness of the muscles of his chest and arms were further reminders of the fact that he could overpower her, sensuously and otherwise and, if the warmth spreading through her was any indication, she might not be able to count on herself to put up much of a fight.

"Your face did get a little burned," he murmured, brushing a rough finger along her cheekbone as spoke.

"Yours didn't."

"I spend a lot of time outside."

"You also spend a lot of time on dance floors," she

teased cautiously. "Is it a hobby of yours or something?"

Locke grinned. "Last night was the first time I danced in months. Since New Year's, I'll bet. It feels pretty good."

"Mmm . . ." She slipped her arms around his neck. "You're being so sweet to Grandma. How come?"

He shrugged self-consciously. "I like her. I don't have any hidden agendas, Josie. That's your department."

"Speaking of hidden agendas." She slid her hand down along his arm and onto his chest. "Don't you ever wear a shoulder harness? Most of the cops I know wear one."

"What are you doing?" he whispered. "Is this for Caroline's benefit, or are you actually coming on to me?"

"Neither. I was just curious." She knew she was blushing as she returned her hand to the nape of his neck. "I like this song they're playing. What's it called?"

"You don't know?"

She shook her head. "It's such a haunting melody. No wonder Grandma thinks there are ghosts here."

"It's called 'Charade.' "

"Really? That's . . . well, it's such a coincidence."

"Yeah." He loosened his hold on her as the music faded into silence. Again he brushed a finger across her cheek. "I think Caroline was right. You should bring lotion to the beach tomorrow."

"Now who's flirting?" The huskiness in her voice

softened the complaint. "Thanks for the dance, Locke." Pulling her gaze reluctantly from his, she noted wistfully, "Looks like Grandma went to bed. To leave us alone. But if you don't mind, I think I'll turn in too. I'm beat."

"Me too." Tilting her chin up with one finger, he brushed his lips across hers. "See you in the morning."

She almost couldn't breathe. Even after he'd walked back into the cottage, she stood frozen to the spot, utterly amazed by how confused a strong, independent woman could get in the right hands. The orchestra began again, and she fought an impulse to call him back onto the deck to identify the song. She had the vague recollection it was about Rockies crumbling or tumbling, which didn't sound very romantic, but in fact it was a stirringly sexy melody. Josie began to move to the beat, then jumped when his voice announced playfully in her ear, "Our Love Is Here to Stay."

"What?!"

"That's the name of the song. You're lyric-impaired or something, right? So I thought I'd help you out."

Josie kept her distance, completely unnerved by the sight of him in his plaid flannel pajama pants and white V-neck T-shirt. He was ready for bed. So, why was he here? And why was he grinning that sexy grin? Didn't he know her grandmother was in the very next room?

"I thought you were tired," she accused warily.

"I'm not ready to go to sleep yet. And there's no

TV. So it was either go over my files or come out here and bother you."

She blushed and nodded. "I can see you're in a silly mood, so—" His words had finally penetrated the sexy fog, and she now began to panic. *Go over my files?* She had assumed he wouldn't be opening the briefcase anytime soon. . . .

"You should go for a walk on the beach," Josie insisted. "The wind's died down, and—"

"No thanks." He chuckled fondly. "Don't look so worried, Josie. I just came out to say good night. I'm not going to attack you or anything."

"Don't be silly. I'm just worried about you. You work too hard."

"I do?"

Josie nodded vigorously. "I want you to promise me you won't give another thought to the robbery, or the jewels, or the reward, or any of that tonight. Give your brain a rest. You'll be fresher in the morning, and then we'll really buckle down to solving this thing."

He studied her, as though instinctively aware that she was trying to manipulate him.

"I'll bet you've been over those dusty old notes a million times anyway," Josie insisted. "I'm just giving you the benefit of my experience. It's dangerous to overthink these kinds of cases. Make your mind a blank, go to sleep, and by morning your brain will probably have the whole thing solved."

He seemed about to retort, then to her surprise he nodded instead. "You're probably right. I do tend to 'overthink' things sometimes."

"So?" She stepped closer hopefully. "You're not going to review your grandpa's files tonight? I guess I'll have to find some way to reward you for that decision."

Locke's blue eyes twinkled. "This sounds promising. But Caroline's in the next room—"

Josie jumped away one second before his hand could land on her waist. "I'm going to reconsider letting you hypnotize Grandma. That's the deal."

He was clearly disappointed, but it only lasted a moment, then he was nodding his head slowly again. "I think it's the perfect solution, Josie. And it's safe— I give you my word. I've had a lot of training—"

"Don't get carried away. I said I'd *think* about it. Now, go keep your part of the bargain and hop into bed. I hope it's comfortable," she added sincerely. "Nighty-night." On impulse, she pecked his cheek, then dashed for the tiny bedroom before he could begin to make any sense of her behavior.

By the time Josie had changed into pink satin pajamas and rubbed more soothing cream into the burns on her cheekbones, Caroline Galloway was fast asleep. The granddaughter felt a stab of guilt at not having said good night or listened to advice on how to win Locke's heart, but she imagined Caroline was content. Probably dreaming of a big wedding or lots of dark-haired, tawny-skinned grandchildren.

"But what you really need is money," Josie informed the sleeping woman lovingly. "And I'm going to do my best to get it for you. Starting with this."

She patted the thick FBI file that she'd retrieved from under the bed, then she moved to an overstuffed chair in the corner and dumped the pages onto the matching ottoman. Warnings of CONFIDENTIAL, DO NOT CIRCULATE and FOR INTERNAL USE ONLY jumped off the pages, giving Josie a thrill that almost rivaled the one Locke had given her that afternoon in the parking lot. Confidential FBI files. To a defense attorney, this was the mother lode.

Just when she thought her pulse couldn't race any more quickly, she began to actually read the first of several official-looking memoranda. "Essential Findings in the Study of Serial Arsonists." *Arsonists?*

"Good grief, Josie, what have you done?" she teased herself nervously. "These are active files. Confidential, active files in an ongoing investigation that he clearly said he wouldn't discuss with you. He's a federal agent, remember? Just because you've kissed him once or twice doesn't mean you can go around stealing this kind of stuff from him!"

She knew she should put it away. *Right* away. But it was simply irresistible, and so she began to devour it instead. "Males between 18 and 27; loners; educational failures; history of criminal activity; medical or mental problems; poor employment records; history of drug or alcohol abuse; dysfunctional families . . . They could be describing almost any of my clients." She smiled to herself. "I could have told them all this. Where's the good stuff—oh!"

A hand had grabbed her across the mouth, silencing her skillfully and immobilizing her without actually causing any injury. After an instant of panic, she

knew it was Locke, and knew further that she wasn't
going to be able to pull off indignation over *this* manhandling—not with official Bureau documents
strewn all over the ottoman and floor!

"What is your problem?" he growled into her ear
as he loosened his hold on her mouth.

"Back off," she whispered. "You'll wake Grandma
up. I didn't know these were the arson files."

"That's your defense? That you meant to steal
something else from me? You're too much, Josie.
This is why you kept making me promise not to work
tonight?"

"What about that?" she demanded halfheartedly.
"You promised—"

"I promised not to work on the robbery."

"Oh, right. Good point." She gave him her best
smile. "This stuff is fascinating, Locke. I'm beginning
to agree with Grandma—your job's pretty impressive.
And so are you."

"And you're a criminal." He was chuckling reluctantly. "Instead of wasting our time profiling arsonists, we should be working on the Galloway gang.
Lying, manipulating, and now stealing. Maybe I
shouldn't have ruled Caroline out as a suspect so
quickly."

"Ha-ha. Wait! Don't take them away." She grabbed
for his wrist as he began gathering the pages. "I want
to read some more. Please?"

"That's not an option." He methodically stuffed
the folder, then eyed the memo that Josie had been
reading. "Hand it over."

"Let me finish this one at least. I was only—" She

grimaced as he began to tug it from her hand. "You're going to tear it, Locke. And you're going to wake Grandma!"

He loosened his grip on the memo. "One way or the other, it's coming with me." Before Josie could catch his meaning, he had thrown her over his shoulder, memo and all, and headed toward the living room.

"Locke Harper!" She had to wail softly, knowing she didn't want Caroline to witness *this*. It could be too easily misinterpreted. Or worse, maybe it really was as sexually ominous as it felt!

He threw her onto the sofa bed and pounced on her, imprisoning each of her limbs with his own. "Now, give me the paper."

"It's yours," she gasped, releasing the memo, which floated onto the floor. "Now get off me, you big jackass."

"Not so fast. I think it's time someone taught you a lesson."

"Oh, really?" She glared confidently. "I may not have a black belt in karate like your Amazon girl-friends, but I have a knee, and I know how to use it, so get off!"

"Relax for a minute, Josie. I just want to talk to you."

She flushed at the husky quality that had invaded his voice. He was pretending to dominate her, and she was pretending to let him, but something else was also happening, and if they weren't careful, the teasing was going to go too far. They were too close, and it was too dark, and there definitely wasn't enough fabric protecting them from each other. The kiss and the dancing had been buffered by two layers of denim. Thin flannel and silky, cotton-candy–colored satin were simply not up to this particular challenge.

"Okay, Locke. You've made your point, and you've had your fun—"

"Are you still giving orders?" he mocked. "Pay attention, Galloway. This is *my* game, not yours. Now, first of all, apologize for stealing my files."

"I was just borrowing them, and you know it."

"Fine. That's how you want to play?" Without further warning, he lowered his mouth to her neck and began to explore it.

Cringing with confused delight, Josie gasped again. "Okay, okay. I'm sorry."

"Too late."

"Locke, cut it out. Oh . . ." She sighed with reluctant pleasure as his lips began to explore her ear. "This is a bad idea . . ."

"This," he corrected, "is a fantastic idea. You smell terrific. And you feel even better."

"That's enough." She tried to wriggle away. "Be reasonable. Grandma's in the next room."

"Then be quiet," he advised. "But keep moving just like that. I like it."

She wriggled again, more briskly so it wouldn't be misunderstood, but she had to admit he was right. Everything was starting to feel much, much too good.

"Are you wearing anything under these?" he murmured, slipping his hand under the waistband of her pajamas.

"Locke, don't."

His fingers grazed down slowly, as though he had all the time in the world. As though he knew her protests were meant only to question, but not stop, his progress. "Nice."

"Grandma's in the next room." How many times was she going to say that before he heard her? she wondered dizzily.

"We're not doing anything," he promised, sliding his hand back up to her chest and cupping a full breast gently. "We're still dressed, right? If she comes in, it'll be like high school all over, right? Didn't your parents ever catch you necking on the sofa?"

"The sofa? Yes. The *fold-out* sofa? No." Josie was giggling in spite of herself. High school had never been like this! And high school *boys* had definitely not been in this league. Locke wasn't sweaty or nervous or out of control. He knew exactly what he was doing, and worse, he somehow knew Josie would allow it, because she'd have to be a masochist to stop him. It felt *sooo* good. And it would feel so much better if she could just be sure Grandma wouldn't wake up. Then she could dare to follow Locke's lead and explore with her own hand. He'd love that, she knew. He'd be inspired, and then there'd be no stopping them. . . .

Locke groaned in her ear as though he'd somehow heard her wayward thoughts. "Relax, Josie. This is so good. So smooth . . ."

"Satin," she explained breathlessly. "I love it too, Locke, but we have to—"

"Just one more minute. Come on, Josie." A raspy edge had invaded his throat. "Man, . . ."

Pushing her pajama top up to her neck, he covered her breasts with fevered kisses, fueled by the tiny gasps of pleasure that Josie didn't even try to stifle. Then he began to move with more authority. More definite need. A need that echoed through Josie, who laced her fingers in his dark, damp wavy hair and began to grind against him.

"Perfect," he growled. "Man, you feel so good—"

"We must be insane!" Wrenching out of his grasp, she jumped from the bed, mortified beyond any and all belief.

"Hey, Josie?"

She turned, expecting to see him needy and apologetic. But his expression was alarmingly matter-of-fact as he warned, "Stay out of my files. Understand?"

That was too much! She wanted to scratch out his sexy blue eyes but didn't dare get close enough to try. Not while arousal and mischief still rumbled in his voice. And so she settled for hissing "Jackass" one last time before escaping to the safety of the bedroom, furious but unwilling to spend even one more second with Locke Harper and his obnoxious teenager-in-heat routine.

At least, Caroline Galloway seemed oblivious to what had happened. Her breathing was even, her expression serene, and her head nestled cozily in a soft, plump pillow. Josie hoped her grandmother was dreaming of her honeymoon. The good parts—or, rather, the romantic ones. *Not* the erotic ones.

As Josie slid into bed, she had to smile at the ludicrous notion of her prim and proper grandparents getting swept up into the kind of frenzied abandon that had claimed Locke.

Of course, Josie herself had been swept up in it too, if only for a moment. That notion seemed equally unbelievable. What a mess! And the next morning, she knew, was going to be even worse.

SIX

Locke was up and dressed by six A.M., anxious to sort through his case file to confirm that Josie hadn't ended up with any confidential documents. He had learned a lot about her the night before, both in bed and out. Lesson number one: He needed to be on his guard against her—twenty-four hours a day. Lesson number two? He needed to spend more time alone with her. Really alone. No chaperons in the next room. It had been a great night, but he had spent hours imagining how much better it might have been.

As he sifted through the documents, his thoughts slowly turned to the arson investigation. His partner would be monitoring it this week, and fortunately, Isaac was the best. Still, if anything big broke while Locke was away, it would be a huge disappointment. He had invested a lot of time in this case, and he wanted to be there when it all finally came down.

Scheduling a vacation had been risky, but with the Greybill jewels beginning to surface, Locke had been forced to do something quickly, before the perpetrator got himself caught and the Harpers never had their chance to prove they could solve a simple robbery-homicide. The arson case took precedence, of course, but it had been going on for three years. Locke himself had been working it consistently for more than a year.

Fortunately, he was becoming more and more adept at predicting the arsonist's moves, to the point where they had missed him the last time only because of accidental but crucial interference by a civilian. In any case, the special profile built by Special Agent Locke Harper predicted that the first week in July would *not* be a time of activity for this particular arsonist.

By seven-fifteen he had finished cataloguing the files, straightening up the sitting area, and ordering breakfast. He could hear movement in the bedroom and suspected Josie was wide awake but unwilling to face him alone. The temptation to be obnoxious was strong, but he promised himself he'd take the high road with her. After all, he owed her.

She finally emerged from the bedroom. Alone. One glance at her face told Locke she had indeed had a frustrating, sleepless night.

Vowing again to be on his best behavior, he greeted her with a warm, pleasant "Good morning."

"Be quiet. Grandma will be out in a second, and you'd better not say anything about anything."

"Anything about anything? That doesn't leave much room for conversation, does it?"

"That's the idea."

"Can I talk about the weather? For example"—he

tried again for an innocent smile—"no sun yet today."

"Just don't talk. Shhh! She's coming."

Caroline stepped into the room, a cheerful smile on her face. "Good morning, children. Locke? How did you sleep? I hope that couch wasn't too uncomfortable."

He crossed the room and kissed her cheek. "I slept better than I have in months. How about you?"

"Oh, the sea air always does wonders for me. But I'm afraid Josie tossed and turned."

He tried his best not to smile, but when the granddaughter's eyes narrowed with contempt despite his effort, he could no longer resist teasing her a bit. "Maybe tonight will be better, Josie."

"Don't count on it." Turning toward Caroline, she announced she was going for a walk, adding, "Do you want me to pick up some tea or juice?"

She had clearly been excluding Locke, but he interrupted anyway. "I already had them send down tea and coffee. And rolls and bacon. They're in the oven, keeping warm."

"Yuck."

"Joselyn Galloway!"

The granddaughter grimaced. "Sorry, Grandma. It's just the thought of bacon—all greasy and piggish and all—disgusts me. I guess I'll just hit the beach. Enjoy your breakfast."

When she'd left, Caroline smiled apologetically. "I've never seen her like this. Maybe it's the wind."

"Probably. Shall we eat on the deck?"

"That sounds lovely." They shuttled the food to a

small patio table and settled back to watch the fog recede. "Josie told me what happened last night, Locke."

His jaw dropped open.

"She told me not to tell you I knew, but I don't like keeping secrets."

Locke shifted in his chair and pretended to concentrate on buttering a roll. The one time when keeping a secret or telling a lie might have been acceptable, and these Galloways chose *it* as an occasion for honesty? "I'm not sure what Josie said—"

"She was quite blunt. She invaded your privacy and rifled through your top-secret papers. Believe me, Locke, I was very disappointed in her. We didn't raise her this way, I guarantee you."

He chuckled with relief. "No problem, Caroline. She was just curious. And she returned them all, so no harm done."

"You're so sweet and understanding. I wish Josie appreciated you more."

"Yeah, me too. More tea?"

"Thank you, dear." Caroline broke off a bit of bread. "This profiling business must be tricky. I mean, the profile says your arsonist is a man between eighteen and twenty-seven, but really, it could turn out to be a female. Right?"

"That's right. In fact"—he pretended to grow suspicious—"where were *you* on May first at ten P.M.?"

After Caroline had laughed in musical delight, he added truthfully, "I'd rather not discuss the case, Caroline. And I'd appreciate it if you and Josie didn't either. I shouldn't have let her get her hands on that information."

"Consider it a closed subject."

"Thanks."

She leaned back in her chair and sighed so wistfully that it actually made Locke's heart ache. "Memories, Caroline?"

"Wonderful ones," she assured him quickly. "I hope you can learn to love this place, Locke. There really are dozens of things to do. When my husband and I were here . . ."

"Go on."

"Well, let's see." She brightened as she spoke of her lost love. "We used to wait for the tide to go out so we could find starfish in the tide pools. We never hurt them, of course," she assured Locke solemnly. "But Jason loved observing nature. And we collected driftwood, and seashells, and bits of colored glass polished by the waves."

"Sounds great."

"When the weather was bad, like this, we would still bundle up and walk on the beach, like you and Josie did yesterday. He used to put his arm around my waist, just like you two did." Smiling mischievously, Caroline reached under her deck chair and pulled out a pair of compact binoculars. "I watched you. It was darling."

Lying, manipulating, stealing—and now he had to add voyeurism to the list? The Galloway profile was getting a little grim. "Did you mention *that* to Josie?"

"In the mood she's in? She'd probably bite my

head off," Caroline said. "But I feel like I can tell *you* anything."

"Well, that's good." *In a weird sort of way,* he added silently.

"One day, when the wind was blowing even worse than yesterday, Jason built me a little driftwood cabin to shelter me from the storm. We used to pretend that those rocks—the ones around the bend that look like an aqueduct?—were a collapsed bridge. And we pretended that the beach was a deserted island. And since the bridge was out, we were stranded here forever. Just the two of us, in our little shelter from the storm." Her eyes clouded. "After the robbery, I remember wishing we really could escape to a desert island for the rest of our lives and never have to deal with strangers again."

"Sorry, Caroline. It was a lousy way to end such a great honeymoon."

"Yes, it was." She raised the binoculars to her eyes. "I don't see Josie anywhere."

"Do you want me to go look for her?"

"If you wouldn't mind. I don't want her to be all alone."

Touched by the concern in her voice, Locke patted Caroline's hand. "Don't worry about Josie. She may be grouchy today, but basically, I think she's one of the happiest people I ever met. She likes her life, and she loves her career. That's good enough for now, don't you think?"

Caroline shrugged. "I suppose. Go and find her though, just to be sure, won't you? And bring her a jacket. She only wore that thin shirt."

"I'll bundle her up, safe and sound. Feel free to watch," he added playfully. *And thanks for the warning.*

Heading down the steep steps, he chuckled to imagine what the prim grandmother would have seen today if Locke hadn't been warned about the binoculars. Not that Josie was likely to let him get away with anything. Still, he'd try, just for the fun of it. But out of range of prying eyes.

Even though Josie was in no mood for games, she had the feeling it might be best to just let Locke get it out of his system. Otherwise, they'd never get the reward, and without the fifty thousand dollars, how was she going to hire a hit man and have the obnoxious agent killed?

Plus, she was freezing, and Locke was bringing her a jacket. In fact, he was holding it out in front of himself like a peace offering. *Very funny,* she complained silently, but aloud she murmured, "Thanks."

"You're welcome." He sat on the sand a judicious distance from her. "Caroline sent me."

"Good. Let's get it over with."

"Huh?"

"I know you have dozens of hilarious one-liners about last night, so go ahead. Get it out of your system so we can get back to work."

"One-liners?"

The fact that he was obviously hiding a smile was more infuriating than one of his grins could ever have been. "Take your best shot, Harper."

"I tried to take it last night—"

"There! That's what I'm talking about!" She jumped to her feet in disgust. "You just *had* to say it, didn't you? Grandma thinks you're 'such a gentleman'—what a crock! Okay, so what else? Don't be shy. Insult me. I deserve it for stealing the file. Go ahead. Take the most twisted, perverted shot you can think of."

"You want me to say something perverted?"

"Absolutely."

"Okay, how's this? Someone's watching us, right now, through binoculars. It doesn't get much more perverted than that, right?"

"Watching us?" Josie spun toward the cliffs and scanned them rapidly. "I don't see anyone. If this is some sort of sexual innuendo, I guess I'm just dense, because I don't get it."

"Check out Cottage Number Four."

"Number four? Grandma? Are you saying . . ."

"Yep."

Josie felt an unfamiliar rush of anger toward her favorite relative. "Does she have some sort of maniacal need to humiliate me?"

"Apparently." Locke grinned sympathetically. "She watched us yesterday. And I'm sure she's watching us now."

"Good grief." Josie shook her head in defeat. "Every time you do something offensive, I have to let you off the hook because my own grandmother does something even *more* offensive. I can't catch a break."

"She's reliving her honeymoon through us."

"Excuse me?"

"We thought she was returning to the scene of the crime, but she returned to the scene of her love affair. She's sitting up there on the deck, remembering tons of details. Unfortunately, in terms of my so-called investigation, she's remembering all the wrong things. But you should hear her. It's amazing. I don't mind being a part of it."

Josie plopped onto the beach and scooped up a handful of sand, sifting it through her fingers for a moment before she turned her gaze back up to Locke's. "She's remembering Grandpa again?"

"Yeah." He studied her carefully. "How about if I tell you all about it up at the big house? They have an espresso bar up there—"

"Warm, frothy caffeine? That sounds pretty good. Let's go." She arched an eyebrow in sharp warning as she stood and brushed the sand from her jeans. "I hate you, you know."

"No problem. With hate like last night, who needs—?"

"Shut up!" she exploded. "Are you going to be a jackass all day? Because if you are, stay away from me."

"You told me to hit you with my best shot."

"That's true." She arched an eyebrow and asked, "Was that it?"

"Yeah."

"Fine. Then don't mention it anymore." *Warm, frothy caffeine . . . warm, frothy caffeine . . .* She continued the silent chant for support until they'd reached the steps, where the need to concentrate on climbing—or, rather, not falling—took over, providing more than enough distraction from her woes.

A double mocha and a huge cinnamon roll were beginning to work their magic on Josie, even though Locke had insisted they sit at the outer edge of the mansion's huge redwood deck "for the view"— and he hadn't meant *their* view of the ocean. He'd meant the Peeping Grandma's view, and Josie knew it.

. "Do you think she's nuts?"

"What?"

"I'm serious. She's been acting so strangely. Like last night. Who orders *clams* for a stranger? Chicken, or maybe pasta. But clams?"

"I liked them."

"I know. But it was still bizarre. Like she's losing it or something."

"No way. She's just sentimental. To a fault."

"There was something my grandfather used to say to her," Josie remembered with a weary smile. "Grandma would say something completely illogical, and he'd say: 'Better be careful. If the men with the nets hear you talking like that, I might not be able to protect you.' Of course," she added dolefully, "I thought he was kidding, but maybe he saw the early signs."

"There's a fine line between brilliance and lunacy, especially where you Galloways are concerned."

Josie sipped in silence for a moment. "You always group me with her. Why? Just because we both have green eyes? We're not really that much alike other than in appearance."

Locke shrugged. "You both lie and manipulate and flirt to get your way. But it's true, you each add your own unique variation—in your case, larceny. In hers, high-tech surveillance."

Josie laughed. "Your stupid files again? You got them back, didn't you? And as for lying, I think that's an unfair accusation. As far as I know, Grandma told only one lie this whole time. That return-to-the-scene-of-the-crime one. And I've only told one."

"One?"

"Yes. I told Grandma I was coming here because I was attracted to you, when it was really all about the reward money."

"Okay, let's count again, shall we? Your grandmother told us she was going to the powder room at the police station, then she ditched us. She told you she had a huge trust fund to pay for your college, then she went broke. She said—"

"Wait! I think that one falls in the category of wishful thinking, not lying."

He seemed to consider that, then nodded. "Okay. She can have a pass on that one. Let's move on to you. You told her I got down on my knees and apologized yesterday—"

"Hyperbole," Josie interrupted sheepishly. "Plus, she knew I was kidding."

"Were you lying when you said you might let me hypnotize Caroline?"

Josie coughed on a sip of sweet liquid, then smiled

in hopes of softening the truth. " 'Lying' is such a strong word."

There it was again, she noted immediately. That flicker of annoyance that could turn those cobalt-blue eyes into blue-black warning signals. She wondered what he was like when he really blew his top, and hoped she and Caroline would make it through the week without finding out.

"Let's talk about something else," she suggested quickly. "Now that the cat's out of the bag on the whole arson mess, why don't you fill me in?"

"I don't discuss active cases with civilians."

Josie bristled. "I'm hardly a civilian! My job centers around crime—"

"Your job is letting criminals go free," he chuckled. "I'd say that makes you the most dangerous kind of civilian there is."

"Making sure that people's rights are protected—" She eyed him suspiciously. "Nice try, Harper, but we're not talking about *my* job. We're talking about the arsonist."

"Actually, we're not."

"Okay, okay." Josie took a deep breath. "I'll make you a deal. Fill me in, just on the major details, and I'll let you hypnotize *me.*"

Locke burst into laughter. "You're too much, Josie. Why would I want to do that? I mean, it might be fun, but what's your angle?"

"Consider it a trial run. You can regress me or whatever, and ask me to remember anything you want, as long as you stay out of my sex life."

"Too late."

She glared pointedly. "Assuming your technique—your *hypnosis* technique—works, and I don't have any painful memories or whatever, I'll talk to Grandma about giving it a try."

His smile faded. "Are you conning me again?"

"No. I promise."

He cocked his head and studied her. "Did you spend a lot of time with her when you were little?"

"With Grandma? Sure. We were practically joined at the hip. She watched me every day while Mom was at work. Then after Dad and Grandpa died, we all moved into Grandma's house." The memory brought an unexpected lump to Josie's throat. "I can't believe she might lose that house after all she did for us there."

"Caroline told me they were killed in a plane accident?"

"Their annual fishing vacation. From the time Dad was a boy, they'd go up to Washington every spring."

"How old were you then?"

"Almost twelve. My brothers were much younger. I think that's why they took it better than I did when Mom remarried years later. *They* got a new dad. I didn't."

"And so your mother and brothers moved down to San Diego to be with him, and you stayed with Caroline?"

"Right. I was almost finished with high school by then, so it made sense." Josie frowned. "You're not going to make me remember the funeral or anything, are you?"

"Of course not. I was just thinking Caroline might

have talked to you about the robbery when you were a little kid. Adults do that, you know. Tell their secrets and fears to infants, or toddlers, or animals."

Josie patted his cheek. "It's a pretty good idea, Harper, except for one small flaw."

"What's that?"

"Grandma didn't have any secrets to tell. I know you think she's a liar, but she didn't lie to your grandfather or to you about the robbery. She just can't remember much."

"And why do you suppose that is? She was an eye—pardon me, *ear*—witness, right? Why does she always draw a blank on the details?"

"I don't know. Maybe she repressed it because it was hideous. Or maybe she's the least observant person on the planet. She was hysterical, you know. She just didn't pay close enough attention to what was going on around her. If she knew something, she would have told your grandfather." Josie eyed him defiantly. "I can't believe you really think she's hiding something. I thought you were just kidding about all that liar stuff."

"I don't think she lied to my grandfather. She was just hysterical, like you said. And now she's getting old, and her memory isn't very good. So I don't think she's lying to me now either.

"All I was suggesting is that in the years between the robbery and now, when she wasn't scared and the memories were still intact, she might have reminisced out loud, without even realizing it, when you were a baby. Told you the story or whatever. I'm sorry I mentioned it."

"No, it's not so lame when you put it like that," Josie admitted. "She used to tell me stories all the time, so maybe it is worth a shot. I mean, it's more likely she would have told Dad when he was a baby, but who knows? Okay, let's give it a try."

"Maybe later. Right now we need to go to the beach and build a cabin out of driftwood."

"I beg your pardon?"

"It's part of our reenactment of Caroline's honeymoon."

"Our reenactment . . . ?"

"She's sick and penniless, Josie," he pretended to scold. "Can't you at least do this one thing for her? Have a heart." Pushing away from the table, he pulled a credit card from his wallet. "I'll go settle up."

As Josie gathered her belongings, she blushed at the nice thoughts she was suddenly having about Agent Locke Harper. How many guys would be willing to let an old woman watch them through binoculars while they pretended to have a romance with an argumentative pest? This was hardly a dream vacation for a hardworking agent. He was *such* a good sport.

Then she realized he had successfully diverted attention from her quest to learn more about the arsonist. Maybe he wasn't such a good sport after all. Maybe he had simply used a penniless, sick woman to manipulate a loving granddaughter!

Thoroughly confused, she decided not to think anymore. She hadn't had much sleep and simply wasn't at her best, and so she'd just buy another mocha, in a beachproof container, and keep a wary eye on her companion. Did it really matter whether he was a good sport or a jackass? What could happen? It was a public beach, right? And on top of that, Grandma would be watching! That was comforting *and* icky, all at the same time, but at least it meant that Locke Harper was going to have to behave himself.

While Locke worked on the beach hut, Josie searched for pieces of driftwood with which to decorate the place. To her amazement, no one had disturbed her earlier collection, and so she had a head start. Unfortunately, some of those pieces now appeared to be borderline phallic, which bothered her, especially in light of the episode on the sofa bed. Nice, hard, smooth pieces of wood? She definitely needed a new hobby. Or a steady boyfriend. Or something.

They quickly discovered that once the fog burned off, morning was the best time, weatherwise, to play on Driftwood Beach. Josie was sure she saw the sun peek through the clouds once or twice, and even if she was mistaken, the absence of wind made the whole place seem much less hostile. Plus, it had a wholesome feel to it that she hoped was dispelling any wayward signals she had sent to Locke the night before.

As though confirming that fact, he actually suggested that they try again to convince her grandmother to join them on the beach. Josie explained patiently that aside from the honeymoon, interactive vacations were definitely not Caroline Galloway's thing.

"I've traveled all over with her," she assured him. "To Grandma, vacations aren't about adventure. They're about postcards."

While he listened in disbelief, she elaborated on the bizarre ritual. "We land. We check in. I go to the nearest shop and buy two dozen postcards. That's it. She's busy for the rest of the trip."

"But—"

"Don't think. Just believe. That's all Grandma wants to do. To write to her friends and tell them what a fantastic time we're having."

"Doing what? If she doesn't do anything—"

"You're thinking again," Josie scolded. "If you want to make this the best vacation ever, just buy her lots of postcards. That's the key."

"Then why am I slaving over this shelter-from-the-storm thing?"

"Because you're a sentimental fool. Get back to work."

It was all true. Josie had once taken Caroline on a whirlwind trip through Ireland and Scotland, only to discover that ten dollars' worth of postcards of the Blarney Stone and Loch Ness were all she'd really needed to provide. Which meant they could have saved five thousand sorely needed dollars, if only Josie had known the truth about Caroline's finances. Maybe there was something to Locke's honesty theory after all!

"I hope you're a great FBI agent, because you could never make a living as a carpenter," she teased him as lunchtime drew near. "One wall in two hours? That's pathetic."

"Carpenters have hammers and nails," he reminded her sourly.

"My grandpa only had his bare hands and Irish ingenuity."

"You could help, you know." He cocked his head to the side, as though suddenly intrigued by the prospect. "Let's see that strong, independent-woman-thing in action."

"The only kind of structures strong, independent women build are *tax* shelters. Let me know when you need one of those. I suppose," Josie added pensively, "I'll be building *lots* of those if we don't get the reward money for Grandma."

"Pardon?"

"It's a way to get money for her so she won't lose the house. I could triple my income overnight working for a tax firm, and I have a standing offer from an excellent one in Sacramento, so . . ."

"That's a depressing thought."

"I know. But there's no way I'm going to let her lose that house." She glanced up toward Cottage No. 4. "I think I'll go check on her. Want me to bring you back a sandwich or something?"

"Sure. And could you bring my baseball cap? It's in my—" He paused to flash a rueful grin. "Believe it or not, I almost gave you permission to open my duffel bag. Not that you need permission, of course. I'm sure you've already ransacked it."

"Don't flatter yourself. So? Sandwiches and a hat?"

"Sounds great. They should have that kind of stuff

up at the coffee shop, so make sure you put everything on my tab. And buy Caroline some postcards on me."

Josie shook her head. "When I told Grandma the FBI was paying for this, I was lying—as usual—so she wouldn't try to spend anything. But *I'll* be reimbursing you every dime, including part of the cost of the cottage."

"That's totally unnecessary." Locke moved closer and insisted, "I don't get to see my own grandmothers too often. Let me spoil Caroline a little. She's making me feel great about myself. Not that you haven't done your part," he added mischievously.

"I'm keeping a list of all these un-agentlike comments, and I'm reporting them to your superiors, so *cut it out.*"

"Whatever you say."

"I'll be back in a few minutes with the food."

"Come here first."

Josie eyed him suspiciously. "What for?"

He shrugged. "I've gone to all this trouble to re-enact her honeymoon. She's going to expect us to kiss each other good-bye and hello, at least. So, come here. I promise I won't enjoy it."

Feeling suddenly shy, Josie stepped cautiously closer. "Just a peck, for Grandma's benefit."

"Sure." He put his hands on her waist and drew her closer. "I promised I wouldn't enjoy this, but I can't guarantee you won't."

Josie laughed despite herself. "Maybe I will, just a little. It'll make up for last night."

He echoed her laughter. "Nice one. Now, where

were we?" Lowering his mouth, he kissed her tenderly, asking nothing in return. "That was for last night. Thanks, Josie."

"You can thank me by not mentioning it again." She smiled to soften the statement. "Now, get back to work. I'll see you in a little while."

As she walked back to the stairs, she savored the taste of him on her lips. What an incredible guy! Maybe she'd been too hasty in swearing off lawmen after all. This one was too good to be true!

Which means you'd better be careful, she counseled herself reluctantly. *After all, he did call Grandma a liar, and I think he called you one too. And he's got some sort of hangup about his grandfather, right? He's not really perfect. He's just a perfect kisser with really blue eyes who happens to know the names of songs and doesn't lose his temper easily. These guys are a dime a dozen, right?*

The fact that he saw her grandmother as a liar really did bother Josie. To make matters worse, she had a nagging feeling that Caroline actually *was* keeping something from them. Josie had defended her to Locke, but in her heart it worried her. Not only was Locke Harper a good kisser, he was also perceptive. And a trained federal agent. And he smelled deception. So what was going on?

Why *hadn't* Grandma remembered more about that night? She was a detail freak! She could remember every dress Josie had ever owned; could describe salespersons in eerie detail, especially when they'd been rude to her; could recite their family history from memory, including birthdays, death days, and every semi-occasion in between. So why hadn't she known anything about the robber?

Josie trudged carefully up the steps, wondering if she should simply confront her grandmother. Maybe there was something going on that the granddaughter had missed! She'd let bankruptcy and heart disease go unnoticed, hadn't she? Why not a fifty-year-old secret clue?

That's crazy, she told herself for the tenth time. *Grandma's the reason you love cops! She has total respect for law and order; she thinks lawmen are heroes and badges mean business; plus, she's a whodunit whiz. She'd never allow someone else to solve a crime that she had the key to. And no matter what Locke Harper says, she'd never lie to a detective without a good reason.*

Which left the obvious question: What was a good reason? For Caroline, that was simple. She'd lie to get Josie a husband or to get a grandchild excused from school to attend a barbecue or to plan an elaborate surprise party. In other words, to help someone she loved. And she hadn't known, much less loved, anyone at Driftwood Point on the night of the robbery except Josie's grandpa.

Which would mean Grandpa stole the jewels and murdered the awful man, and Grandma's lying to protect him, she grumbled silently. *Which of course is beyond ridiculous. So what's left? Nothing, right? She wouldn't lie to the authorities. Period.*

It made sense except for one gnawing detail—the panic. The muted but unmistakable fear that showed on Caroline's sweet face whenever the mansion or Greybill or the jewels were mentioned. Why, why,

why? Why was she afraid? Who or what would threaten a sweet old lady?

"Not an old lady though," Josie announced to the world in general as she scaled the last of the seventy-seven steps. "She was a beautiful young bride who had never been more than thirty miles from home before that honeymoon. Threatening her would have been a walk in the park for an experienced felon."

That had to be it!

Sprinting the last hundred yards to the cottage, Josie cursed the fiend who had dared to terrorize her grandmother. They would make him pay! He was still alive—the jewels that had recently popped up in Reno attested to that. But he was also a dead man, because Josie Galloway was going to strangle him with her bare hands!

"Josie! I didn't expect to see you until dinnertime."

"Cut the act, Grandma. Locke told me about the binoculars."

Caroline giggled. "He's building you a beach hut. Isn't that the sweetest thing you ever heard?"

"It's first class," Josie agreed. "And guess what? He's hungry and wants a sandwich yesterday."

"Oh, dear! You'd better hurry over to the snack bar."

Josie flopped onto the couch, kicked her shoes off, and buried her face in her hands. "I'm in no hurry. He can starve to death for all I care. I've got more important problems."

"Problems?"

"That's right. My own grandmother doesn't trust me. My favorite client in the whole world has been lying to me. So, here I am. Completely disillusioned and feeling like a failure. And"—Josie couldn't help but allow a genuine sob to enter her voice—"there's only one thing that can make me feel better."

Caroline Galloway immediately joined her, sitting on the edge of the sofa and staring in profound dismay. "What on earth are you talking about?"

Tears streamed unexpectedly down Josie's cheeks. "Tell me what happened to you fifty years ago. Please, Grandma?" She embraced the older woman tenderly. "Someone threatened you, right? I can't believe I've been this blind! Someone told you they'd hurt you, or hurt Grandpa, if you talked to the police, and so you pretended you didn't know anything. I'm so sorry, Grandma! I'm so sorry I didn't figure it out sooner."

Caroline began to stroke Josie's sunstreaked curls. "Where on earth did you get this silly idea? Did Locke suggest it, because if he did, he's wrong. And frankly, I'm a little disappointed in him for upsetting you this way."

"Upsetting me?" Josie wailed. "What about you? You've had to live with this, night and day, for fifty years—"

"Live with what? A bad memory? For heaven's sake, Josie, I really think you need to go lie down. You're overtired. Because of the wind, I imagine."

"The wind?"

"It kept you up all night," Carolyn soothed. "It

affects everyone differently, you know. Locke says he slept like a baby—"

"Would you forget about Locke Harper for ten seconds? We're talking about *you*. My wonderful, perfect grandma. And about the murderer. He killed a man, right before your eyes, then threatened to do the same to you, or Grandpa, if you squealed."

"Joselyn Galloway! Do you really think I'd protect a despicable stranger? And a murderer to boot? Don't you know me better than that?"

Josie wiped her tears and studied Carolyn's face anxiously. "Level with me, Grandma. Please? I'm not just your granddaughter. I'm your lawyer. I won't tell anyone what you say to me. It's privileged information, and I'll take it to the grave."

Caroline sighed as she took her granddaughter's tear-streaked face between her hands. "No one threatened me. I'm not protecting some awful criminal. I promise."

"Then, why don't you remember?" Josie groaned. "You remember everything else! Why is this such a blank for you?"

"I was dizzy. Pregnant with your father, as it turned out. Someday you'll understand how many changes your body goes through at times like that. I simply wasn't myself."

"Pregnant? After two days of sex? I suppose that's possible, but I doubt you'd have had dizziness and other symptoms that quickly."

"What can I say? I was dizzy. Nine months later, more or less, I had a handsome son. I'm not a doctor, but . . ." Caroline shrugged her shoulders in dismissal. "These are private circumstances, and I don't want to discuss them with my granddaughter *or* my lawyer."

Josie smiled warily. *More or less?* "Okay, I'm officially in shock. You're saying you might have been pregnant before the honeymoon? Which means you and Grandpa—"

"I said no such thing, Joselyn Ann. I only said I was dizzy. That's nothing to be shocked about."

"Okay, I'm adjusting." Josie managed a shaky grin. "Just answer one more question, okay?"

"Certainly."

"Did you and Grandpa ever have sex on the beach?"

"That's enough."

"Seriously, Grandma, I need to know this. My whole definition of appropriate behavior is changing—"

"I said that's enough." Caroline laughed. "You tease me just the way your father used to. It's what I love best about you, you know. The way you remind me of him."

"I know." Josie hugged her ferociously. "I'm just *sooo* glad to know that murderer didn't threaten you. He didn't even talk to you, right?"

"I've never spoken to a murderer in my life, and I hope I never will. You, on the other hand talk to them all the time."

"Those are *alleged* murderers," Josie reminded her. "Once they're declared guilty, I'm out of their lives in a flash."

"I should hope so." Caroline peered out the window anxiously. "Go and get my binoculars, won't you, Josie? I can't see what Locke is doing."

"He's starving to death." Josie laughed. "If you're okay, I should probably go get that sandwich for him. And some postcards, of course."

"What a wonderful idea! I've almost run out of stationery."

Josie hugged her again, this time with as much tenderness as she could muster. "Do you have any idea how important you are to me?"

"Yes," Caroline answered softly. "I believe I do."

"Promise me you'll never lie to me?"

"Why would I lie to you?" Caroline smiled. "It would be like lying to a part of myself."

"Okay, then. Don't lie to me or to your arm or to your leg. We'd all be plenty upset if you did."

Caroline laughed admiringly. "Go and feed Locke now. And tell him not to plant such silly ideas in your head anymore."

"He didn't—" Josie stopped herself and summoned an innocent smile instead. If Grandma was finally ready to admit that the Special Agent wasn't so special after all, who was Josie to interfere? It was healthy. Plus, it would make things easier when he went back to his silly arson investigation and Josie went back to . . . well, whatever.

ou like steamy passion, mystery and intrigue,
autiful sophisticated heroines, powerful
nning heroes, and exotic settings then...

EBRA
OUQUET
ROMANCES ARE
OR
OU!

*Special
Introductory
Offer!*

Get 4 Zebra
Bouquet Romances
Absolutely Free!!

$15.96 value – nothing to buy, no obligation

THE PUBLISHERS OF ZEBRA BOUQUET

are making this special offer to lovers of contemporary romances to introduce this exciting new line of novels. Zebra Bouquet Romances have been praised by critics and authors alike as being of the highest quality and best written romantic fiction available today.

EACH FULL-LENGTH NOVEL

has been written by authors you know and love as well as by up-and-coming writers that you'll only find with Zebra Bouquet. We'll bring you the newest novels by world famous authors like Vanessa Grant, Judy Gill, Ann Josephson and award winning Suzanne Barrett and Leigh Greenwood—to name just a few. Zebra Bouquet's editors have selected only the very best and highest quality romances for up-and-coming publications under the Bouquet banner.

YOU'LL BE TREATED

to tales of star-crossed lovers in glamourous settings that are sure to captivate you. These stories will keep you enthralled to the very happy end.

4 FREE NOVELS As a way to introduce you to these terrific romances, the publishers of Bouquet are offering Zebra Romance readers Four Free Bouquet novels. They are yours for the asking with no obligation to buy a single book. Read them at your leisure. We are sure that after you've read these introductory books you'll want more! (If you do not wish to receive any further Bouquet novels, simply write "cancel" on the invoice and return to us within 10 days.)

SAVE 20% WITH HOME DELIVERY

Each month you'll receive four just-published Bouquet romances. We'll ship them to you as soon as they are printed (you may even get them before the bookstores). You'll have 10 days to preview these exciting novels for Free. If you decide to keep them, you'll be billed the special preferred home subscription price of just $3.20 per book; a total of just $12.80 — that's a savings of 20% off the publisher's price. If for any reason you are not satisfied simply return the novels for full credit, no questions asked. You'll never have to purchase a minimum number of books and you may cancel your subscription at any time.

GET STARTED TODAY –
NO RISK AND NO OBLIGATION

To get your introductory gift of 4 Free Bouquet Romances fill out and mail the
enclosed Free Book Certificate today. We'll ship your free books as soon as we
receive this information. Remember that you are under no obligation. This is
a risk-free offer from the publishers of Zebra Bouquet Romances.

Call us TOLL FREE at 1-888-345-BOOK
Visit our website at www.kensingtonbooks.com

FREE BOOK CERTIFICATE

YES! I would like to take you up on your offer. Please send me 4 Free Bouquet Romance Novels as my introductory gift. I understand that unless I tell you otherwise, I will then receive the 4 newest Bouquet novels to preview each month FREE for 10 days. If I decide to keep them I'll pay the preferred home subscriber's price of just $3.20 each (a total of only $12.80) plus $1.50 for shipping and handling. That's a 20% savings off the publisher's price. I understand that I may return any shipment for full credit–no questions asked–and I may cancel this subscription at any time with no obligation. Regardless of what I decide to do, the 4 Free Introductory Novels are mine to keep as Bouquet's gift.

BN070A

Name _____

Address _____

City _____ State _____ Zip _____

Telephone ( ) _____

Signature _____

(If under 18, parent or guardian must sign.)

Orders subject to acceptance by Zebra Home Subscription Service. Terms and Prices subject to change.
Order valid only in the U.S.

If this response card is missing,
call us at 1-888-345-BOOK.

Be sure to visit our website at
www.kensingtonbooks.com

BOUQUET ROMANCES
Zebra Home Subscription Service, Inc.
P.O. Box 5214
Clifton NJ 07015-5214

PLACE
STAMP
HERE

SEVEN

Two hours later Locke met Josie at the bottom of the steps, where he hastily relieved her of two of her three bulging shopping bags. "If I'd known you were going to buy out the restaurant, I would have come with you. What the heck's in here? A banquet?"

"Wait until you see." Josie dug into the remaining bag and produced a soft pink sweatshirt embroidered with a gray Driftwood Point logo. "Isn't it great? And there's a matching windbreaker . . . where is it?" She rummaged again, then eyed the larger of Locke's two bags. "I guess it's in that one. With the beach blanket. The other one has the sandwiches and some drinks."

He wasn't smiling, and so she quickly assured him, "I paid for these myself, so don't get all bent out of shape."

"You went shopping? Is that some sort of disease with you two?" He shook his head as though disgusted. "You leave on a quick errand, then disappear for hours?"

Grateful that she had dropped the rest of the packages off at the cottage, along with lunch for her grandmother, Josie decided to humor him. "I guess you get cranky when you're hungry. Let's spread out the blanket and eat. I got you a hero sandwich," she added mischievously.

Locke finally smiled. "Cute, Josie. Did you get post-cards?"

"Of course. And sunscreen. And . . ." She reached into her bag again, pulling out a navy blue sports cap that also bore the Driftwood Point emblem. "A souvenir for you, even though you probably don't want to remember this vacation."

"It's had its moments." He smiled.

They spread the lightweight rainbow-striped blanket near the water's edge, then chatted as they ate. Josie was certain she could get him to talk about the arsonist eventually, but for the moment settled for details about his family. No siblings but lots of cousins, all of whom lived on the East Coast. Were they a tight-knit family? Josie couldn't tell for sure. But she knew that Locke's relationship with his grandfather had been a close one, at least. When he talked about family, he talked mostly about that agent-turned-judge. It was sweet. And sad. And it made Josie appreciate Caroline all the more.

"Okay, now for the pièce de résistance." Josie smiled. "Have you ever been in love?"

"No."

She was amazed by the curt reply. Not *I came close once or twice* or *I thought I was once, but I was wrong . . .* Just *no?* Almost as though he'd been asked the question once too many times and was tired of it. Or defensive about his inability to love. Or maybe he'd been hurt so badly that he couldn't bear to talk about it! Josie had to know. "Touchy subject?"

"Not really." He seemed to realize she wasn't going to let it go. "It's no big deal, Josie. I actually think my experience is typical. In high school and college, dating was just a game. In law school, I concentrated on working hard, because I was determined to join the FBI, and they only take the top students.

"The last thing I needed was to have my career sabotaged by an unplanned pregnancy or a disease or some other disaster. So, I became pretty conservative in my dating habits. At least"—he grinned wryly—"as conservative as my partner and his wife will let me be. They're as bad as Caroline when it comes to matchmaking, so I'm sure my days are numbered."

Josie was nodding eagerly. It all made so much sense! "The last thing you needed was to have your career sabotaged by a woman. You weren't going to make the same mistake your grandpa made. That explains a lot."

"I think I liked you better when you were cross-examining me. This amateur-psychologist routine is lame."

Josie refused to be dismissed. "You know I'm right. You're afraid of love, because it might make you a less effective agent. But the good news is, when you solve the Greybill case, I think you'll get the monkey off your back and you'll be ready for a real relationship."

"What a relief. Thanks, doc." He began to gather up the sandwich wrappers and bottles. "Speaking of solving the case, I'd like to take a couple more hours this afternoon to finish searching those rocks for hiding places. And"—he paused to glare—"I wouldn't mind some help this time, if you can tear yourself away from your beachcombing."

"I helped!"

"You checked out three crevices. As opposed to the hundreds I did."

"I use a different technique." She shrugged. "I study the entire cliff, from a criminal's point of view, and identify the most likely spots."

"Well, if anyone has a criminal's point of view, it's you, so I guess that makes sense," he said with a laugh.

"A good profiler needs to be able to put herself in the perpetrator's shoes, right?"

"Now you're a profiler?" He chuckled again. "Nice try, counselor. But I'm on vacation, remember? No shop talk. Let's go for a walk instead."

As they headed around the bend toward the rocky arch, Josie asked cautiously, "I hope this isn't another sore subject, but did you give up on building the hut?"

"Me? Give up? Never." He pushed up the brim of his hat and grinned. "I finished it just before you got back."

"What? And you didn't tell me? Here!" She stuffed packages and tennis shoes into his hands, then sprinted barefoot along the sand until the structure came into view.

It was a little lopsided, and no one over the age of four could have stood upright in it, and it probably couldn't survive much rain or high wind, but Josie had to admit it was a pretty good effort. Somehow he'd managed to brace the walls just right and had even left a little rectangular gap in one to serve as a window. "This," she pronounced when he caught up to her, "is darling. Do you think Grandma can see it from our cottage?"

"Yeah. Just barely. She said they built theirs over in this area, so I wanted to be as accurate as possible." Unfolding the blanket, he spread it as a floor. "Come on inside."

"It's great," Josie enthused as she settled into place. "I'm impressed, Locke. What other secret talents . . . ?" She grimaced sweetly. "Never mind."

"You read my mind." Sidling up to her, he insisted, "We have complete privacy in here, you know. The Peeping Grandma can't see us, and no one else is crazy enough to hang out on this godforsaken beach."

The hand he placed on her shoulder was warm and reassuring. "Lie back and relax, Josie. I want to talk to you."

"Are you going to hypnotize me?"

"Maybe later. Right now I want you fully functioning—"

"Wait!" She edged away warily. "I know I gave you the wrong impression last night—"

"Last night was great," he corrected her. "You and I are great together." He kissed her gently, and when she responded with tentative interest, he again urged her to "lie back and relax."

There was only one problem, but it was a big one,

and so she reluctantly pushed on his chest until finally he lifted his head enough to stare down at her, his eyes blazing with frustration. "What now?"

"This is your worst nightmare, Locke. Don't you see that?"

"Are you crazy? This is great."

"You're letting your investigation be sabotaged by a woman. First Grandma did it to your grandfather. Now you're letting it happen again."

His eyes darkened until they were virtually unreadable. "More amateur psychology?"

"Think about it."

"If you don't want to kiss me, just say so." He sat up and stared out at the ocean. "Leave my grandfather out of it. I wish I'd never told you about him."

Josie sat up beside him and patted his muscular forearm. "I'm sorry, Locke. I actually do want to kiss you, you know. I just don't want you to blame me later for distracting you from the case."

"I'm not my grandfather."

"And I'm definitely not Grandma. But there are some similarities."

When he turned to look at her, she was relieved to see that the storm had passed. In fact, he looked almost sheepish. "I'm not usually so touchy. Sorry, Josie."

She brushed her lips across his. "Let's pretend I never opened my big mouth."

"Actually, I think you were right."

Josie winced slightly. "I was?"

"Yeah. You've been right all along. I came up here to prove I could do what Grandfather couldn't do.

To prove I could be more professional and focused and all that crap. I criticized him for being easily distracted by a green-eyed girl in a beach resort. Then I come up here and I'm worse than he ever was. *Everything* here distracts me! The wind, the music, the damned haunted mansion, this stupid hut, and, of course, you—the biggest distraction of them all. Like I said," he added wryly, "I can usually concentrate on a case even if there's a pretty girl involved in it. But when it comes to Driftwood Point, I'm just as much a loser as he was." He cocked his head and studied her smile. "Did I say something funny?"

"You said something darling," she corrected. "Don't you see, Locke? You've got it all backward."

"Huh?"

"You *thought* you came up here to prove you could be a better agent than your grandpa, but really, you were trying to prove just the opposite."

"I was?"

"Absolutely. You wanted to prove that no one, not even a first-class focuser like Locke Harper, could do a better job on this case than he did. He was your hero, right? I think you've accomplished just what you needed to accomplish with this trip. You've proven once and for all that he was the all-time best."

Locke was hanging on her words as though they were lifelines. "You're saying that somehow, subconsciously, I wanted to mess this up from the start?"

"Exactly!"

"That makes a lot of sense," he admitted with quiet relief. "Why else would I have gotten this distracted? I mean, let's face it, I've seen *much* better beaches.

Spectacular ones, in fact. And I've had to deal with *much* more uncooperative witnesses than Caroline."

"And of course," Josie finished coolly, "you've dated *much* prettier women, right?" She scooted away before he could react. "Fortunately, I'm not in a beauty contest here. I'm trying to save my grandmother's house. And now that you've got your personal life squared away, I'd appreciate some help."

"Josie—"

"If you really want to be like your grandfather, then help Caroline Galloway. That's what *he* did fifty years ago, and that's what he'd do today if he were here."

Locke grabbed her by both shoulders and insisted, "I never said—"

"Forget it!" She flushed and added weakly, "Can't we just drop it? I meant what I said, Locke. I need to help Grandma. That has to be my priority—my *only* priority. You don't want her to lose her house, do you?" She pulled free and crawled quickly out of the shelter, then turned and tried to smile. "I think I'll go check on her. Want me to bring you anything when I come back?"

"No, thanks. Just leave the packages, and I'll bring them up in a while."

"Okay. See you." As she straightened and began to walk back toward the steps, she looked up toward the cottages and waved, just in case Caroline was watching. The last thing she wanted was for her grandmother to see that her darling Josie had gotten her feelings hurt.

The warnings Josie had given to the older woman about Locke's motives rang in her ears. *He's got an agenda . . . it's all about his relationship with his grand-father. . . .* If only she'd taken her own advice! Now Locke had closure, and Caroline probably had *fore*-closure. And Josie had an ego bruise the size of the Greybill mansion.

Get over it, she instructed herself grimly. *This isn't even about you. It's about Grandma, so pull yourself together.*

"Hey, Josie!"

She turned reluctantly and allowed him to catch up to her. He was carrying the packages, which meant he intended to tag along—hopefully with a minimum of small talk and *no* humiliating apologies. "Look over there," she said as evenly as she could manage. "I think the sun's coming out."

"Listen, Josie—"

"Guess what? I've decided you're not a jackass after all."

His smile was guarded. "I'm something worse?"

"No. You're a fantastic person. And I'm a fantastic person too. Unfortunately, we're oil and water. It's not anyone's fault, it's just the way it is."

"We weren't oil and water last night."

"Last night was fun." She nodded. "But like you said, it was pretty juvenile. Straight out of high school." She cocked her head to the side in what she hoped looked like genuine apology. "Sorry, Locke, but that's how I see it."

He was doing his expressionless routine again, and it was really beginning to bother her. Was he angry? Relieved? Confused? Who could tell? "Say something," she demanded finally.

"If I say something, you'll twist it around and use it against me. That's probably why your grandfather and father were the quote-unquote strong, silent type. They learned to keep their mouths shut around Galloway women."

Josie was impressed. Apparently, either she or her grandmother had made some offhand comment about the two men's personalities, and it had stuck with Locke. Maybe it had even made him a little jealous? That evened things up between them a bit, at least. That, plus calling his lovemaking "juvenile," was probably the best she could hope for in this mess.

"Too bad though."

Josie arched an eyebrow, intrigued by the smell of manipulation in his pseudosympathetic tone. "What's too bad?"

"I was all prepared to tell you about the arson investigation—just to make up for that imaginary insult back at the hut. But now I guess I'll be silent instead."

She grinned in defeat. "You win. Can I read the confidential files too?"

"Sure. Knock yourself out."

"Okay, you're officially forgiven. Let's go."

"One more thing."

Ugh, she thought to herself. *The dreaded apology.* But she wanted to see those files, so . . . "Okay, let's get it over with. I'm the prettiest-sexiest-sweetest-whatever woman you've ever met. Blah, blah, blah. Anything else?"

"Yeah. You're also the most obnoxious," he said, scowling. "Now, get over here and let me put my arm around your waist, so Caroline doesn't think we're having problems." When Josie had followed his instruction, he added quietly, "We're not, are we? Having any problems, I mean?"

"We're still oil and water," she reminded him ruefully. "But maybe we can salvage a friendship out of this mess if we both behave ourselves from here on out. I'd like that, Locke."

"Yeah, so would I."

"So . . ." She could barely keep a casual tone to her voice as they began to stroll up the beach together. "Tell me about our arsonist."

The Greybill mansion, for all its checkered history, was easily the most luxurious and inviting place Josie had ever visited. The upstairs rooms had been converted, ten years earlier, for guest occupancy, while the entire downstairs had been thrown open to the public at large, including travelers who strayed from the highway in search of a nice meal and regulars of all ages from the nearby town. The massive redwood deck, which served both the elegant formal restaurant and the more casual coffee shop and snack bar, had a live band and dancing five nights a week, and reputedly did a brisk business, especially on weekends.

Another outdoor area that had been made accessible to visitors was the veranda that figured so prominently in Caroline's memory of the night of the murder. Paved with slate and lushly decorated with ferns and fragrant vines, its view was one of the more breathtaking ones the mansion had to offer.

The actual scene of the crime—the victim's study—

had been refurbished with overstuffed chairs and an ornate card/chess table, along with several small desks stocked with Driftwood Point stationery. This was the spot Josie and Locke chose for their arsonist discussion, but first she needed to satisfy her curiosity about the older unsolved crime, and so she took a few minutes to study the scene.

"I like it in here. Too bad it's haunted."

"Right. Want to see where they found the body?"

Josie nodded. "Grandma says a brandy bottle had spilled right on the floor next to him."

"Right. Someone surprised him, apparently. They forced him to open the safe, then hit him over the head. He landed next to the bottle, not vice versa."

"What other clues were there?"

"None. If it had happened today, with our advances in forensics, we could probably have turned something else up, but in those days it was fingerprints, re-creations, and witness accounts. Plus, some of the servants may have contaminated the crime scene by trying to straighten up before Grandfather arrived. It sounds like things got out of hand for a few minutes right after the body was discovered."

Josie examined the area with a practiced eye. "Even with those French doors open, I don't think Grandma could have heard much from the veranda. Especially if the wind was howling, like it was last night. I guess you've been right all along," Josie admitted thoughtfully. "Hypnosis is really our only shot at getting that reward."

Locke nodded. "According to Grandfather's notes, there wasn't any wind up here the night of the murder. She *must* have heard something, then suppressed it because it was too painful. I have a list of everyone who was here that night, and even if she remembered just a voice, it would help. Some of the suspects had distinctive accents—"

"Suspects? Wasn't everyone a suspect?"

"In a sense, yes. But some had more reason than others to want Greybill dead."

"According to Grandma, he was an awful human being."

"That was the consensus," Locke confirmed. "I'll show you the list later if you want."

Josie smiled in genuine appreciation. He seemed so relaxed and content, presumably because he was at peace with his memories of his grandfather and no longer felt a need to compete with so honorable a hero. And she suspected Locke was also relieved that his relationship with Josie had evolved from a rocky, dead-end romance to a comforting and possibly long-lasting friendship.

"Okay, I'm ready." She curled up in a plush green corduroy chair and, after he had positioned a second armchair directly in front of her, she gestured for him to begin. "What kind of fires does our guy set? Where does he set them? Do we think it's a money thing, or strictly psycho? Does he send little anonymous notes to the newspapers taking credit? Is he—"

"Josie? I know I'm supposed to be silent, but if you want answers . . . ."

She grinned and nodded. "Just start at the beginning."

"The beginning was probably in his childhood."

"Wait! Do we know for sure it's a he?"

"No. But my instincts—and the official profile—tell me he is." He leaned closer and explained. "Female arsonists are usually motivated by things that happen in their personal lives: feuds with parents or siblings; soured relationships; neighbors with barking dogs. That sort of thing. And so the fires are usually close to home, in residential areas. This guy hits warehouses and bus depots. Places like that."

"Because he's motivated by . . . ?"

"That's the key. If we could figure that out, we'd have him."

"Warehouses and bus depots," she mused. "Has anyone gotten hurt in one of his fires?"

"Not yet." Locke paused, as though carefully framing his next remark. "I have other cases, with seemingly more dangerous perps. But there's something about this guy that makes me want to catch him soon. Before he kills someone. Each fire is more daring than the next in some respect. Either he doesn't care if people get hurt or he's actually intrigued by the prospect of it."

"You need to catch him right away, then." Josie snuggled farther into her chair. "Tell me about the profile."

"The official line is that our guy likes the attention. The power. He sets a fire, and suddenly, people are evacuating buildings, sirens are wailing, fire engines and cop cars are speeding to the scene. All because of him. That's a fairly typical motive in cases like this."

The official line . . . Josie felt a rush of admiration

for her handsome new friend. He was questioning the profile. Because he knew instinctively that this guy was not a composite or paint-by-the-numbers crook. This perpetrator was an individual and probably a brilliant one. It would take an equally brilliant lawman to catch him. And Locke was hot on the trail!

"No more questions?" he prodded.

"Thousands. But first tell me why *you* think he sets fires."

"Didn't I just do that?"

She pretended to study her neatly manicured nails, as though she had all the time in the world, and after almost a full minute she heard him begin to chuckle. It was a great sound. A sexy sound. She remembered just how sexy it had sounded the night before, on the sofa bed, when he'd been teasing her, just before things went crazy.

"I think there's a religious angle."

"Hmmm?" She had to force her wayward thoughts back to the present. "Religious? You think he's a priest or minister or something?"

"No. At least, not of any recognized religion. My theory—" He flushed self-consciously. "Feel free to tear it apart, by the way. You'll be in good company."

"Your partner doesn't agree with you?"

"Isaac? He's okay with it. But the agent in Chicago who's actually coordinating the investigation—"

"Chicago?"

"The fires started there three years ago. Although our guy probably began during childhood by setting small ones—trash cans, leaf piles, and, of course, bowls of cornflakes." He paused to grin belatedly at her cereal-arsonist joke. "All very typical."

"When did he move to L.A.?"

"About a year ago."

"And the agent in Chicago thinks the guy's looking for attention? But you think it's religious? Explain that."

"He's looking for attention either way. But Jessica thinks it's all about—"

"Jessica?" Josie's eyes narrowed. "Let me guess: She's one of those sharpshooting, karate-chopping Amazons you talked about on the way up? The ones that are so strong and independent?"

"Yes."

She tried to fight a wave of jealousy, but it was too strong. "Are you having an affair with her?"

"Where did *that* come from?" he chuckled. "If I was having an affair with her, would I have been making out with you last night?"

"So? The affair ended? Why? Because she didn't buy your religion theory?"

Locke shook his head. "I don't answer trick questions. Do you want to talk about the case or not?"

"Sorry. I know it sounds silly, but since I've given up lying, I have to admit that I despise Jessica with every fiber of my being."

"It's a big club." He grinned.

"Really?" Josie laughed with relief. "Okay. He sets the fires in warehouses and bus depots, not churches. But you think they're religiously motivated? Does he burn crosses or something?"

"No. Just whatever debris is handy."

"But they're religious, which means what? Are they *near* churches?"

"Sometimes." He studied her intently. "Does that make sense to you? I mean, that's why everyone else has a problem with my theory, so it surprises me that you'd come up with it so fast. Because"—he took a deep breath—"if the fires are religiously motivated, wouldn't it make more sense for him to set them *in* a church?"

"If he was part of an organized religion, then yes. He'd set one in a rival church, maybe—to destroy it. Or he'd set it in his own church to grab headlines for it. But you said he's not part of any organized religion, right?"

"Go on."

She stared into his eyes, hoping to discover what it was he wanted her to say. It seemed so important to him. Almost crucial. Because no one else had gotten it so far, and he needed "confirmation."

And then suddenly she knew. Not because she saw an answer in his eyes, but because she saw flames. Beautiful cobalt-blue flames . . .

Locke waited impatiently, certain that of all the people in his life, Josie Galloway was the one with enough imagination and instinct to make this jump His partner had tried. Some of the others hadn't even bothered. And the "Amazon" in Chicago had trashed his profile so completely that he'd felt the fallout all the way in Los Angeles.

"Just say it out loud, Josie. Say whatever comes into your head. It's more of a . . . well, a leap than a deduction."

"Okay, I'll give it a try." She moistened her lips. "Arsonists love fire, right?"

"Right."

"But your guy doesn't just love it. He worships it. Right?"

"Yeah." He felt an unexpected lump in his throat. "That's what I think, at least." He shook his head. "Last winter I arrived at one of the scenes before the fire was completely out, and it flamed up a little in front of me. And in the background was a church. I was impressed with the combination—flames plus spirituality. It was actually kind of inspiring. I didn't think much more about it at the time."

"But when you reviewed the details of the other fires, you started noticing churches in the vicinity. Different denominations?"

"Right. No pattern, except that a person standing in the right place could always see the flames and the church simultaneously. And so at first I thought it was a tribute. To God. A way of calling attention to the churches—"

"But it's really the *contrast* he wants people to notice. The church is pale and lifeless in comparison to the glory of the flames, right?"

Locke exhaled sharply, hoping she hadn't noticed how keyed up he'd become. "That's the theory. What do you think?"

"I think it's clearly correct. And not just because I hate Jessica."

He wanted to assure Josie she was more beautiful in every way than the heartless Amazon, but couldn't afford to distract her yet. He still needed to hear her ideas, which hopefully would continue to mesh with his own. "Want to hear the best part?"

Josie nodded eagerly.

"When I went back and checked out the dates—"

"Religious holidays!" She literally jumped out of her seat. "Good grief! How can they doubt you now? It's ironclad, isn't it?"

"More or less. Unfortunately, there are *lots* of religious holidays once you start taking minor ones into account. Throw a dart at a calendar and you're bound to hit one. Plus, the arsonist is sporadic. For example, nothing on Easter this year. That made me look like a fool, especially after I kept people from traveling to be with their families, all on the strength of my hunch."

"Like you said, there are lots of religious holidays. The guy can't cover them all."

"But Easter? That's a pretty big one."

"To Christians, sure. But our guy isn't a Christian or Jew or Muslim. He's more of an old-fashioned pagan. A fire worshipper."

"Yeah. That's what I said too. But it shook my confidence."

Josie settled back into her chair. "Since you're here instead of there, I'm guessing there are no major religious holidays this week?"

"Right. At least, none that I think might push his buttons."

"On the other hand." She studied him quizzically. "Fourth of July's pretty big, isn't it?"

"But completely secular."

"Hmm . . ."

He grinned as he watched her go through the same thought processes he'd wrestled with before making his travel arrangements. "It's clean, Josie. No religious angle at all. Halloween and Valentine's Day and even St. Patrick's Day have overtones, but not the Fourth. It's just party time."

"With *fire*works."

"I thought about that. Our guy probably loves it. With so many other people celebrating—religiously or otherwise—he can afford to take the night off. See? Let other people light the matches for once. Maybe he'll set off a few Roman candles himself for fun. But he can afford to stay in the background, and so he will."

She nodded slowly. "I guess you're right."

"You 'guess'?"

"I could argue it either way, but then . . ." She smiled impishly. "That's what I do for a living, remember? I take whichever side of an argument works for me, and then I create reasonable doubt. But in this case your side works just fine for me, so why bother?"

"But you could argue the other side? You could make a case for him specifically targeting the Fourth of July? How?"

Josie shrugged. "Back off, big fella. I'm sure you're right. Secular holiday. Someone else lighting the matches. Roman candles, et cetera, et cetera. It makes total sense."

"Listen, Josie." He leaned forward and growled, "The last thing I want to hear from you on July *fifth* is that you had some sort of feeling he'd set a fire on the Fourth, so spit it out now."

"Okay, okay." She jumped to her feet again. "Watch. Here's me, on the Fourth of July. Looking up at the sky saying 'Ooo, ahhh.' If I were your guy, I'd find that slightly annoying."

"You would?"

"Sure. We *call* them fireworks, but they aren't really fire, right? Not fire in the sense of flames. Flames consume and threaten and rage and engulf. Compared to them, fireworks are a joke. Harmless, colorful little explosions in the sky are like . . . well, like false gods. Yet all those crowds stand around and admire them. If I were your guy, I'd want to give them some of that 'contrast' you referred to earlier. But"—she touched his cheek reassuringly—"I'm sure you're right."

"Yeah. Me too."

"So? What now? You can hypnotize me if you want."

"Maybe later." He was running it through his head just to be sure. False gods? Did that actually make sense, or was she just a great saleswoman? Like she said, this is what she did for a living: created "reasonable doubt" where no doubt existed.

So why was he suddenly having doubts?

"Locke?"

"Huh? Oh, sorry." He grinned sheepishly. "Did you say something?"

"I said we should buy Grandma a souvenir. We could give it to her tonight at dinner to soften her up for the hypnotism."

"You think she'll be afraid?"

"Maybe a little, but she really wants to help. And she trusts you so completely, it's scary."

"We should buy her a souvenir," he agreed. "Since you're the shopper, I delegate my authority to you. Pick something nice and charge it to my account."

"You don't want to help pick it out?" Josie shrugged, as though to say it was his loss. "I'll probably browse for hours again, so maybe you should just head back without me. Play cards with Grandma or something."

"Good idea."

He walked her to the row of stores that lined one side of the mansion, then stood and watched until she disappeared into a dress shop. It would have been fun to go with her and buy her something to wear dancing that evening. Or better still, a revealing piece of lingerie to wear later, in the sofa bed. But he didn't have time for such indulgences at the moment. He had to get to his cell phone and make some backup plans with Isaac, just in case Josie's version of reasonable doubt turned out to be more reasonable than his own.

EIGHT

Josie had three reasons for wearing her sexy red dress to dinner that night, even though she and Locke were now officially just friends. The first was the best: Grandma had agreed to go up to the mansion and dine on the redwood deck. It was a wonderful breakthrough and would pave the way for the hypnosis, especially after they gave her the souvenir that Jose had found hidden in a cluttered corner of the Driftwood Point Gift Shoppe.

The second reason for wearing the slinky tube dress could be summed up in one word: Jessica.

The third reason was a practical one. Josie simply hadn't been able to find anything more alluring despite having tried on every fancy dress Driftwood Point had to offer. She had wanted something with a full skirt for dancing, and a skimpy, eat-your-heart-out bodice for blatant showcasing. But nothing had had that special something that oozed from every fiber of the crimson bombshell dress.

And when Locke walked out of the bathroom and saw her, she knew she had made the right choice, because his cobalt-blue eyes rolled right out of his head and across the floor to land at her feet. Or at least, it almost seemed that they did.

"Wow. Did I buy that for you?"

"This old thing? I've had it for months, but I never had an excuse to wear it until now." She moved her leg to demonstrate the slit that ran up her right thigh. "Are you sure it's not too much?"

"*You're* too much," he corrected reverently. "And you . . ." He turned to Caroline and smiled. "You look great too. Did I buy *that* one, at least?"

"Of course not. Galloway women don't allow men to buy them clothes unless they're related—or at least engaged. I bought this dress for myself the afternoon I 'ditched' you and Josie at the police station."

Josie's laugh was tinged with pride. "You really do look nice, Grandma. Green is your color."

"*Our* color. Although I can see why Locke likes you in red." She beamed at the agent as though he were her long-lost son. "I was beginning to worry about you, spending all that time on your cell phone this afternoon. But here you are, looking dashing and relaxed, thank goodness."

"On the phone?" Josie frowned. "Who were you talking to, Locke?"

"Relax. It wasn't Jessica."

"How could it be? I put a contract out on her hours ago." Stepping up to him, Josie smoothed the lapels of his white dinner jacket. "You're a hunk, by the way. I love this look."

"I wouldn't want to embarrass the Galloway women.

Shall we go?" Crooking an arm toward each of the females, he gallantly escorted them to their ride.

"Do you have any idea how well this dress fits you?" Locke pulled her closer as they swayed to a gentle love song. "You're driving me crazy."

Josie blushed at the feel of his clearly aroused body. "I love dancing with you. You're so easy to impress."

"Yeah, well, you don't know the half of it. Even when I'm alone, you're on my mind these days."

"Like when you were on the phone?"

He kissed her cheek, then moved his mouth to her earlobe. "What perfume are you wearing?"

"Seriously, Locke. Who called you? Was it Isaac? Is there a new development I should know about?"

"Yeah." His hand wandered from the small of her back to caress her bare shoulder. "I'm developing a serious crush on you. Later tonight I'll show you—"

"Sorry, I graduated from high school ten years ago. I don't do the grandma-in-the-next-room cha-cha anymore. Give me a call when you grow up and get your own place."

Locke chuckled against her neck, and Josie thanked heaven he didn't know how fantastically erotic it felt. "You're in luck. I do have my own place."

"But it's in L.A."

"No, it's down on the beach. Three walls and a roof. An ocean view, and hopefully a view of the stars." His tone grew desperate. "We need to be alone at least once before—"

"Before you go back to Los Angeles and I go back to Sutterville with my impoverished grandmother?"

"Nice job of taking the romance out of it," he complained.

"Somebody had to. Oil and water is bad enough—but oil and water separated by three hundred miles? That's pretty hopeless."

"So, why'd you wear the dress?"

"Pure vanity," she admitted cheerfully. "Oh, dear, the song's over. Wasn't that unfortunate timing?"

"Actually, it was 'Volare,' " he grumbled as he led her back to the table just as their main course arrived. "Have you noticed that all we do on this vacation is eat?"

"Be nice. Ask Grandma to dance again."

"Why not? That's my job, right? Platonic escort to the world." As he held her chair out for Josie, he warned softly, "This isn't over."

She pecked his cheek, loving the fact that he couldn't do anything about it. This was fun! The original plan—her throwing herself at him while he pretended to resist—had been all wrong. This felt much, much better.

"You two make the most stunning couple," Caroline informed them proudly. "The entire room was staring at you while you danced."

"Take a vacation from matchmaking, Grandma." Josie turned to Locke. "Want to hear a cute story? According to my father, Grandma used to bug him about getting married all the time. He was a confirmed bachelor for years. Then, when he was almost thirty-two, he finally brought home a fiancée. She was older than him by about six years, and she was very 'sophisticated.' Which is a Galloway code word for *bitchy.*"

"Joselyn Ann!"

"So Grandma freaked and went into emergency matchmaking mode."

"And found your mother for him?" Locke guessed.

"Right."

"That's enough." Caroline eyed Locke sternly. "Don't believe a word of this. I'll admit, I counseled my son against marrying that woman because it was clear she didn't want children and I knew he'd be a wonderful father. But the rest was fortuitous."

Locke looked to Josie for the rest of the story. "Go on."

"Grandma hired a pretty grad student from a nearby university to come and cook dinner every night. This girl had it all—looks, brains, charm, and, best of all, fertility. And lucky for all of us, Dad fell like a ton of bricks. As planned."

Caroline was shaking her head emphatically. "Even if I had wanted to plan such a thing, my husband— Josie's grandfather—would never have allowed me to interfere like that. And my son would never have allowed himself to be manipulated."

"Right," Josie drawled. "That's why Dad made the same toast each and every year on their wedding anniversary: *For an arranged marriage, this has turned out pretty well.*"

Tears pooled in Caroline's eyes. "He loved to tease me, just like you do. How I miss him."

Locke patted Caroline's hand. "I'm sorry you had

to lose them both so suddenly." Tilting her chin up a bit, he observed quietly, "My grandfather wrote in his journal that your eyes got even greener when you cried. I didn't think it was possible, but it's true."

"He was very kind to me."

Perfect timing, Josie decided, motioning for the waiter who was hovering nearby with a brightly wrapped gift. "Look, Grandma. A present. From Locke and me to you. I hope you like it."

"A gift for me? You shouldn't have! Thank you, children." She pulled at the ribbon, then carefully folded back the tissue paper and opened the box. Once again tears filled the emerald eyes. "Oh, Josie . . ."

The granddaughter's own eyes began to sting as her grandmother tilted the water-filled globe, allowing sparkling sand to drift gently over a miniature re-creation of Driftwood Point's rocky arch. "We hope it brings back only good memories, Grandma."

"I can almost see him standing there," Caroline sobbed. "What a perfect gift." She hugged Josie, and then turned to Locke and threw her arms around his neck. "Thank you so much for bringing me here. I needed to come back. I needed to clear away all the bad memories so that the good ones—like this spot on the beach—could grow stronger."

"I'm glad I brought you too. I can't imagine this trip without you and Josie."

Josie smiled encouragingly. "If you really want to clear away the bad memories, Grandma—"

"Wait, Josie." Locke glanced at her uneasily. "Maybe we shouldn't push this."

She smiled at the protective attitude. "Like grand-father, like grandson. Locke's dying to solve the case, Grandma, and for that he needs to hypnotize you. But he doesn't want to upset you. And neither do I." She took the older woman's hand and squeezed it. "Will you give it a try?"

Caroline bit her lip. "Would we have to go to the veranda to do it? Or that awful man's study?"

"Absolutely not," Locke assured her. "We can do it anywhere you want. Back at the cottage, or even back in Sutterville, in your own living room, if that's what you want."

"Oh, no! We mustn't go home yet." She glanced nervously toward Josie. "You were against hypnosis before."

"I know. But it's the only way. And Svengali here is going to demonstrate it first—using *me* as the human guinea pig. If anything bizarre or embarrassing happens, we'll cancel the whole thing."

Caroline seemed to carefully weigh this informa-tion before surprising them both with an enthusiastic "It's a wonderful idea. But can we wait until tomor-row?"

"Tonight would be better." Locke smiled encour-agingly. Wouldn't you like to get it over with?"

Surprised and annoyed, Josie kicked him sharply under the table. "Don't rush her. Tomorrow would be fine, Grandma. Isn't that right, Locke?"

"Whatever."

Caroline beamed as she played with the dazzling sand globe. "I have a feeling tomorrow's going to be the best day yet. Maybe the sun will even come out.

That would give Josie a chance to wear the bikini she bought today."

"You're pimping again, Grandma."

"Josie!"

"You bought a bikini?" Locke's expression brightened considerably. "This vacation just keeps getting better and better." Sliding back his chair, he stood and took Josie's hand. "They're playing our song."

It was "Charade" again, and Josie was tempted to give him another kick. "It's Grandma's turn."

"You two go ahead. Please? I want to look at my present and remember your grandfather."

"Nice job picking the souvenir, Josie. Caroline loves it. Look at her." Locke grinned when Josie pretended to be bored. "What did I do wrong this time?"

"Why were you pressuring my grandma to do the hypnosis tonight instead of tomorrow?"

He hesitated, wondering if he should tell her he might be leaving in the morning, assuming Isaac could make the travel arrangements quickly enough. But it was more likely that Locke wouldn't be catching a plane until later in the afternoon, so there was time to break it to her later. He'd be back in a day or two, of course, but he knew she'd still be annoyed, and that was the last thing he wanted just then. Playing "oil and water" was one thing during the daytime, but the moonlight, the music, the red dress, and the female herself had put him in the mood for something a little more tangible. And a lot more erotic.

And he had a feeling she wanted it too. Even as

she pouted, her body was molding itself against his. For Caroline's benefit? Maybe partially. But the "charade" couldn't account for the fact that her skin was almost feverish and her fingertips kept playing in the hair at the nape of his neck.

"You know what I think?" he murmured seductively. "I think we're both frustrated. One minute we're fighting, next minute we're dancing, and half the time we can't remember if we're pretending or not. But last night neither of us was pretending. And tonight—"

"I agree. No more pretending."

"Really?"

"It made sense at the beginning, but we've come a long way since then. So, I'll be the first to admit it. I find you unbelievably attractive."

Locke exhaled in relief. "Great. I thought you were going to play hard-to-get."

"No. But I'm also not going to play easy-to-get. I've known you for three days. We live three hundred miles apart. And you're a cop. So I need to take it slow." She blushed as she added, "After this week's over, if you still want to date me, you know where I live. But for now, let's just stick with the friendship thing, okay? I'm just not the type to have a fling, even with a terrific guy like you."

He knew she was right. He also knew this was one of those compliments that didn't feel like a compliment at the time of receipt. She was saying she might like to build a relationship with him, even though she'd sworn off cops. In the morning, that would make him feel like a fine human being. But at the moment, with her spilling out of her red dress eve-rywhere he looked—everywhere he touched!—the compliment didn't quite work.

"The dress was kind of a low blow," he complained again.

"Good. I owed you one for calling me ugly this afternoon."

Locke chuckled with her. "So? What do you want to do tonight? I'll be too frustrated to sleep, I know that."

"Me too," she admitted. "How about letting me read your grandpa's journals? I'd love to see Grandma through his eyes. And I'd like to get to know him better, since he means so much to you."

"Sure." Locke kissed her cheek before leading her back to their table. "You'll let me know if you change your mind about mindless sex, right?"

"You'll be the first." She giggled. "And, Locke?" She traced a gentle line along his jaw with her fin-gertip. "Thanks for understanding."

Josie changed her mind about mindless sex a dozen times that night, especially when she cuddled up against Locke on the couch and read through the pages of the journal. It could have been Locke him-self who'd written it. There was the same blend of drive and caution; of intellect and romanticism; of ambition and honor. All that was missing was Locke's sense of humor. Without it, Josie imagined that the grandfather's life must have been almost unbearably solemn and unrelenting.

To his credit, Locke didn't try, even once, to seduce her. In fact, she could tell he was affirmatively avoiding any such conduct. Which of course made him even more maddeningly attractive. He had changed into gray sweat pants and a white T-shirt, and patiently played round after round of solitaire by her side for hours while she read. She in turn wore her new pink warm-up suit in hopes of dispelling some of the confusion the red dress had created. But the confusion was there, and though neither mentioned it, each knew that they were missing something sensational in exchange for the promise of something that might be even better.

Josie was the first to awaken the next morning, and she blushed to find herself snuggling against the handsome agent's chest. His dark hair was tousled, his face needed a shave, and his breathing was steady and steadying. Somehow, the combination was irresistible to Josie and, with a mischievous smile, she started to slide her hand under his T-shirt in hopes he would awaken in the same amorous mood. Then she remembered Caroline and flushed as she jumped from the couch.

"What?" Locke stirred, opened one eye, then closed it and winced as though in pain. "Did I sleep like this the whole night?"

"We slept like that."

"Yeah?" He stretched his arms toward the ceiling and yawned loudly. "Did I miss anything else?"

"I was naked for an hour or so," she teased. "But it got cold, so I put these back on."

"You're obnoxious twenty-four hours a day, I see."

Josie smiled and moved toward the kitchen. "Hurry and use the bathroom while I start the coffee. And try to look innocent when Grandma comes out."

"That won't be too tough, thanks to you."

"You're welcome."

He paused in the bathroom doorway. "Did I get any calls?"

Josie put her hands on her hips. "You're expecting more calls? What's going on?"

"Let me wake up for a minute, will you? I'll tell you when I come back out."

Tell me what? She stomped her foot in frustration, then immediately chastised herself, remembering how much frustration he had cheerfully endured the night before. She had no right to give him grief in return. But she'd get to the bottom of this telephone business, with any luck before Grandma woke up and further complicated things.

"I think I've been pretty patient."

Locke took a sip of coffee before grinning sympathetically. "You really have. It's a side of you I've never seen before."

"Well, I thought I owed you a little slack. But now tell me who you've been conspiring with behind my back."

He couldn't put it off any longer. And fortunately, he no longer dreaded her reaction to the news of his departure. They were clearly going to have time to do the hypnosis before he left; they'd have at least a day to follow up on any clues once he returned; and thanks to her, it wasn't as though he was running out 'the morning after' a night of heated lovemaking.

But just to be on the safe side, he wanted to do a little damage control first. "I have two things to discuss with you, Josie. Both are important."

"The phone thing first, please."

"I would, except I don't mind if Caroline hears about that. This other thing is a secret from her for the time being."

She was visibly intrigued by the idea of a secret but still seemed to suspect he was tricking her somehow, so he explained, "The phone call is no mystery. I'm just expecting an update from Isaac. I'll fill you in more later, but first things first." He took her hand in his own. "I have some money saved. It's not quite fifty thousand dollars, but it's a start, and—"

"Good grief, Locke. Don't do that. It's sweet, but it's not necessary. I told you, if this doesn't work out, I can bump up my income easily by doing tax law." She squeezed his hand in gentle appreciation. "Thanks though."

"I've been looking for an investment," Locke continued stubbornly. "Caroline's house looked pretty solid to me. Great neighborhood and all that. She could live there, rent free, and take care of the place for me until the time is right to liquidate it."

"You should have told me this last night," she murmured. "It's the sweetest, sexiest pickup line I've ever heard."

"It's not a line," he objected quickly. "No strings attached. I think it's a good idea for everyone. And I think your idea—quitting criminal defense to do tax law—is a lousy one. It's a waste of your talent."

"You are *so* darling." Josie scooted from her chair into his lap. "Just like your grandpa. Rescuing Grandma from the big, bad world. I could eat you up."

Locke smiled with relief, certain now that, while she'd be disappointed over his trip to Los Angeles, she'd also be forgiving. "If the hypnosis doesn't work, I'd like to talk to Caroline about the money right away. The sooner we start making the arrangements, the better."

Josie cuddled against him. "I'm not going to let you do it, silly. Grandma's my responsibility. But I'm going to adore you forever for making the offer."

He felt an all-too-familiar rush of frustration. "Come on, Josie! Let me help. I'm not going to just sit by and let you give up your career. That makes no sense."

"You're not going to *let* me?" She stirred and sat up straight. "What does *that* mean?"

He coughed uneasily. Suddenly, this wasn't going so well. "You're missing the point. You want a guy to appreciate your strength and independence. That's what I'm doing. I'm being supportive of your career."

She was on her feet in an instant. "This is your idea of being supportive? Of acknowledging my in-dependence? You're doing *exactly* what those other guys tried to do. You're trying to rescue me from reality. To protect me from the big, bad world. That helpless-victim stuff works for Grandma. It doesn't work for me."

"You're officially impossible," he growled. "Forget I said anything. If I want to help Caroline, I will. It's got nothing to do with you or your paranoid damsel-in-distress delusions."

"Help Caroline with what?" a voice demanded from the bedroom doorway.

Josie sprinted to embrace her grandmother. "We were just having a stupid quarrel about nothing."

"It was about me," Caroline corrected haughtily. "I'm the helpless victim, am I not?"

Locke wanted to help Josie even at the risk of being accused of rescuing her again, but the sound of his cellular phone ringing inside his duffel bag distracted him. It also caught the attention of the two females and in that sense could have been a welcome diversion had he not known it would cause more problems than it would solve. "I have to get that. But first—Caroline? We weren't fighting about you. Just take my word for that."

Leaving the room would just postpone the inevitable, so Locke flipped open the phone right there in the living room and listened as his partner detailed the travel arrangements the Bureau had made for him. After a few oblique questions, he thanked Isaac, closed up the phone, and returned Josie's stare as evenly as possible. "Where were we?"

Her brilliant green eyes narrowed. "Are you going somewhere?"

"Yeah, just for a day or two. I'll be back before you know it."

Caroline seemed to have completely forgotten that she was miffed. "Did the arsonist set another fire? I know you're not supposed to talk about your cases, but—"

"It's fine," he assured her. "There's been a new development, and I'm going to fly down and check it out. No big deal."

Caroline frowned in disapproval. "You shouldn't have to work on your vacation. Can't the other agents handle it?"

"In other words, you don't want your matchmaking interrupted? Nice try, Caroline," he teased. "Thanks for worrying, but believe me, I want to go. This could be the break we've been waiting for."

"Locke?" Josie interrupted sharply. "Could I speak to you for a moment in private? On the deck?"

He winced to think she needed to be out of her grandmother's hearing before chewing him out. Was it going to be *that* explosive? Up until then her tirades had been short and fairly sweet. This, on the other hand, did not sound good. "Excuse us, Caroline. Have some coffee. Josie made it, and it tastes great."

Following the granddaughter out onto the deck, he rapidly prepared his defense. If careers were important to her, she should respect the fact that this was part of his. Plus, she herself had planted the idea in his head that he needed to be in Los Angeles for this particular holiday. And they were already in the middle of a fight, so the timing couldn't have been better.

Then she turned toward him, and he was surprised to see only mild annoyance in the green eyes. Maybe this wouldn't be so bad after all. "Is something wrong?" he asked innocently.

"You've known about this trip since yesterday? Why didn't you mention it earlier? We could have been making plans all this time instead of wasting time arguing."

"That's true. I'm sorry."

She shrugged and then, to his amazement, actually smiled. "I'm not going to let it ruin the trip. Are we flying out of Sacramento or San Francisco? I think Sac would be faster, but since no one consulted me—"

"Wait a minute! What's this 'we'? If you think I'm bringing you and Caroline, you're nuts."

"Grandma on a stakeout?" Josie laughed with delight. "You're right, that's nuts. Luckily, I think she'll be fine here alone. We won't be gone for more than two days, right?"

"Josie . . ."

"Don't say I can't come!" She sandwiched his face between her hands and gushed, "Please, Locke? I promise I won't get in the way. I go on ride-alongs all the time with the Sutterville cops, and I know just how to act. I won't even remind you to read the bad guy his rights. I'll just be a silent observer. Please?"

"No." He couldn't help but chuckle. "I thought you'd be mad that I was going."

"You *have* to go. You've been working on this case

for a whole year! And you have to take me with you.
I'm the one who thought of the whole false-gods theory in the first place, right?"

"It's too dangerous, Josie."

"I'll wear a vest. And I'll follow your instructions
to the letter. And I'll be so grateful." She curled her
arms around his neck and murmured, "You can show
me where you live. And we won't have Grandma in
the next room to cramp our style—"

"Wait a minute." He laughed. "I thought we were
just friends."

"Us? *Please.* Are you forgetting the sofa bed?"

"We're oil and water."

"We'll take turns being oil," Josie assured him impishly. "You first."

Against his better judgment, Locke pulled her
against himself and growled, "If I'm even going to
consider this, I'm going to need something a little
more explicit than that."

"How's this?" She laced her fingers behind his
head and dragged his mouth down to hers.

She was hungrier than he could have dreamed possible, as though three straight days of arousal were
suddenly being unleashed in one hot, relentless,
probing kiss. Locke responded in kind, grinding
against her as his hand moved under her thin T-shirt
to greedily fondle her breasts. When she gasped with
delight, he dared explore lower and was stunned
when she actually followed suit, sliding her hand inside the elastic waistband of his sweat pants. Her fingers curled around him, and then she stroked him

with a firm, hard stroke that made him groan out loud, "Okay, you can come."

To his groggy amazement, she continued to move in rhythmic anticipation, and he realized just how caught up in the kiss she'd become. He also realized that he had to be the one to restore sanity—*temporary* sanity—to the situation. "Josie, honey, listen for a minute. Josie? We have to stop. Your grandmother could walk out here any minute."

Josie gasped for a breath, then nodded and released him. Leaning her cheek against his chest for support.

"Sorry, Josie."

"Mmm . . . I guess I got carried away. From all the excitement. And you. You're so sexy sometimes. Thanks for the reality check."

"Believe me, it killed me to stop you."

She looked up at him and smiled gratefully. "It was supposed to be a preview not the main event." Craning her neck, she peeked around the corner. "I guess Grandma's giving us privacy. She probably thinks we're arguing. But I don't want to argue, Locke. And I don't want to take advantage of you. If you really don't want me to come with you—"

"You can come."

She cocked her head inquiringly. "Because of the kiss or because you think I'll be a help?"

He grinned and admitted, "Because of the kiss."

"I can live with that."

"Can you live with my rules?" he countered quietly. "For example, you can brainstorm with me and Isaac, and I'll even go over the strategy with you, but when and if the call comes, you'll stay at my place."

"But—"

"Take it or leave it." He almost weakened in the face of her disappointment but knew he had to be firm. "This isn't a game, Josie."

"Fast cars, guns, badges, bad guys?" She grinned mischievously. "It's *definitely* a game. The question is, are you any good at it?" Rising up on tiptoe, she stared into his eyes, then murmured, "Oh, my gosh, you are."

The reverence in her tone amused him. "So? Are you coming with me?"

"I wouldn't miss it for the world. Let's go break the news to Grandma."

To their surprise, Caroline insisted she didn't mind being left alone for a few days with her memories as long as they got the hypnosis out of the way before they left, and so Josie was soon stretched out on the bed, smiling shyly up at Locke. "I'm all yours."

"Okay. Just relax." He had placed a metronome on the nightstand and now released the switch, carefully adjusting the steady click of the mechanism. "In a minute we're going to count backwards together. But first I want you to try to make your mind a blank. Don't evaluate what's happening. Just let it happen. You'll remember everything when I wake you up, and you can analyze it to death then."

"I thought I was supposed to picture someplace I

feel safe and happy," Josie complained. "Are you sure you've got this right?"

Locke smiled across his subject toward her grandmother, who had pulled a deck chair up to the bed and was watching intently. "Has she always been this obnoxious?"

"Okay, okay." Josie brushed a curl from her forehead then closed her eyes. "I'm making my mind a blank."

"Good. Now we're going to count backward. Softly and slowly. We'll start at ninety-nine. You'll listen to me, and I'll listen to you. When you get too tired to count, just go to sleep.

"All you have to do is listen to me, Josie, and I'll do the rest. My voice is the only thing that matters right now. Just listen and relax and . . ." He studied her for a second, then grinned up at Caroline. "What a pushover."

"Already?" Caroline whispered. "Without even counting? Is that normal?"

"It's rare, but it happens."

"Well, she hasn't been getting much sleep," the grandmother reminded him. "Poor thing is exhausted."

He wanted to explain that a hypnotic state was different from sleep, but it didn't seem important. In fact, nothing in the world seemed important to Locke except Josie. She looked so peaceful and so exquisitely beautiful, he almost believed he was falling in love with her at that very moment. With her mind empty and her guard down, she was docile, vulnerable, and amazingly irresistible. Completely under his power. Guided by nothing but the sound of his voice.

He squirmed slightly, remembering the debate they'd had during the trip up the mountain. She had accused him of wanting a helpless female to protect, not a strong, capable woman to be his companion and equal. At the time it had seemed ludicrous beyond belief. But now . . .

"Locke?" Caroline whispered. "Is something wrong?"

He shook his head. "We'll get started now. Josie? Can you hear me?"

"Hmm?"

"Listen to my voice, Josie. I'm going to ask you a few questions. Is that okay with you?"

"Yes."

"Good." He flushed, wishing he'd prepared some questions in advance. Usually, he made a few innocent, noninflammatory inquires just to be sure everything was going well, then proceeded to the purpose of the session. But even innocent questions seemed awkward with this particular subject. There was so much he wanted to know that he didn't have the right to ask, and so much she might not want to share with him yet.

"Okay, Josie. Let's talk about some of the vacations you've taken with your grandmother. Do you remember anything special?"

Josie smiled. "We went to Ireland last year."

"That's good. How old were you then?"

"I was twenty-five. Almost twenty-six."

"Good, Josie. Go back ten years. Do you remember when you were sixteen?"

"I remember . . . hmmmm . . . I remember all the sailors."

"The sailors? Where did you see sailors?"

"In San Diego."

Locke took a moment to exchange smiles with Caroline. "Let's go back further now. Do you remember when you were only five? Do you remember being in Grandma's kitchen?"

"Making pie?"

"Right. Making pie. What sort of pie?"

"It wasn't sorta pie," Josie corrected. "It was *all* pie."

"Pumpkin pie?"

"Grandpa hates pumpkin pie." Josie seemed disgusted that Locke had made such a suggestion. "It makes him get measly."

"Measly?"

"An allergic rash," Caroline whispered. "It's so cute that she remembers that."

"Okay, Josie. You're doing fine. I have one more question. Did Grandma ever talk to you about her honeymoon?"

When Caroline gasped, Locke grimaced apologetically. "I thought Josie told you we were going to do this. Are you okay with it?"

Caroline bit her lip but nodded for him to proceed.

"Okay, Josie. Try to remember. Your grandparents took a trip called a honeymoon, and—"

"I'm bremembering," she assured him. "But it's so, so sad."

"The honeymoon? Why is it sad?"

"Grandma always cries about it, so we shouldn't talk about it anymore. But we can talk about the pie, but"—a no-nonsense tone crept into her little voice—"*not* the pumpkin one."

Locke had to struggle not to laugh at the childlike instruction. "I liked talking about the pie too. But let's talk about the honeymoon again for a minute. Okay?"

Josie scowled. "I'm not s'posed to talk about bad stuff. Only good stuff."

"Really, Locke," Caroline protested. "You're upsetting her. I want you to wake her up this instant."

Locke wanted to explain that Josie wasn't in any danger. But the whole point was for Caroline to feel comfortable with the process and so, as much as he wanted to spend a little more time with his fascinating young subject, he announced, "Okay, Josie. Do you remember when we talked about all the sailors you saw when you were fifteen?"

"They were so cute."

"I'll bet."

"One of them called me 'baby.' "

"That's fine. Do you remember going to Ireland with Grandma last year?"

"Yes."

"Good girl. Now we're going to count again, but this time we're going to count forward to three. And when we say three, I'll snap my fingers and you'll wake up. You'll remember what we talked about, and you'll feel relaxed and refreshed. Okay?"

"Yes."

He felt a rush of anticipation at having the old Josie back. She would have some hilarious observations about the sailors and the pie and would probably browbeat him for upsetting Caroline. He was looking forward to every minute of it.

Relieved to know that he didn't really prefer docile and vulnerable after all, he counted to three and brought his sleeping beauty out of her trance.

"Hi, Josie. Welcome back."

"Hi." She smiled shyly. "That wasn't so bad." Then she turned to Caroline and murmured, "You're so pale. Did something happen? I thought it went well."

"It went great," Locke insisted. "But if you're worried, Caroline, we can postpone——"

"No!" The older woman laughed apologetically. "It confused me to see her like that, I think. She was so childlike. But I'm not at all worried. In fact, I'm anxious to begin."

Josie sent Locke a puzzled look, then shrugged and hopped off the bed. "Be my guest, Grandma. It's fun."

Locke described the procedure again, knowing that it served the additional purpose of helping the subject relax. Then he reminded Caroline to make her mind a blank and to listen to the sound of his voice. "Let's count together softly now. Ninety-nine . . . ninety-eight . . . ninety-seven . . ."

Caroline's eyelids drooped, but to Locke's trained eye there was nothing relaxed about it at all. He also noted that her tone of voice as she counted backward was strained and exaggerated. Caroline Galloway was up to her old tricks, manipulating the situations, with no intention of allowing herself to be hypnotized. But why?

Because she's afraid to go under, he reminded himself. *The memories scare her. But she doesn't want to disappoint you and Josie, so she's going to reenact some melodramatic hypnosis scene instead.*

As usual, his reaction to her manipulative conduct was mixed, because he knew she was doing it out of love. Still, it annoyed the heck out of him, and he wasn't going to put up with it for long. He wouldn't embarrass her by confronting her, but he'd make the "session" as short as possible.

"Okay, Caroline. I'm going to ask you a few questions now. Is that all right with you?"

"Yes," she moaned.

"Is she okay?" Josie whispered. "She sounds different."

"She's fine." It amused him to realize that the usually perceptive granddaughter was falling for this hokey routine so easily. "Okay, Caroline. Do you remember the robbery at Driftwood Point? You were on the veranda and you heard noises. Do you remember what kind of noises?"

"Voices," Caroline crooned. *"Two* voices."

Her zombie act was becoming more aggravating by the second, and Locke had to take a deep breath to keep his own voice steady. "Good. Anything else?"

"I hear a woman's voice. She sounds very, very angry."

Locke felt his patience snap. It was bad enough to con them, but to feed them useless information? To make them believe they should suspect a female?

That was simply too much. "Okay, Caroline. That was very helpful. Now I'm going to wake you up. One, two, three." Ignoring Josie's hiss of protest, he snapped his fingers briskly. "Nice job, Caroline. Are you feeling okay?"

She put her hand to her forehead. "I'm a little dizzy, but I'm sure I'll be fine. Did I say anything useful?"

"How come she doesn't remember?" Josie grumbled. "I think you screwed that one up, Svengali."

"Believe me, it was a classic," he countered. "Now let's get going. We have a plane—and an arsonist—to catch."

NINE

As it turned out, they didn't need to travel far to catch their plane. The FBI had arranged to have them picked up at a small airstrip only thirty minutes from Driftwood Point. The accommodations impressed Josie, indicating once again that the magnitude of this case, and of Locke Harper's role in it, were not to be underestimated.

If only it had been a plush private jet, she might have been tempted to follow through on the amorous part of their bargain right away, but the no-frills military transport, while adequate, was not exactly an airborne love nest. Even if it had been, she had the feeling Locke was busy psyching himself back into warrior mode—he was even wearing a shoulder harness now!—and she was the last female on earth to want to stop something as exciting as that.

He was so wrapped up in the case that it startled her when he abruptly asked permission to ask a "personal question."

"Sure. Anything you want."

Locke smiled at the invitation. "I was just curious.

You talk so much about cops and sailors and other assorted 'gunslingers.' How many times have you actually been in love with . . . well, with guys like me?"

"The closest I've ever come to a hunk like you is in a movie theater," she assured him playfully. "And the closest I've ever come to being in love is there too." When he looked puzzled, she reminded him, "I told you all about that on the drive up the coast. My relationships have all been disasters. I'm lucky if I make it past the first date, much less all the way to love.

"I came close once. Ten whole dates—my personal best. With a detective—one I really thought was okay with my job. But one day, when I was scheduled to interview an inmate at Vacaville, he said . . ." She paused, surprised at the rush of anger that could still accompany this memory after seven long months. "He said, 'This is where I draw the line, Josie.'"

Locke studied her carefully. "Vacaville is where they put some of the crazies, right?"

"That's right. Do you have a problem with that?"

"No, ma'am. You'd fit right in."

Josie tried to smile. "Good save. Unfortunately, this guy really went off on me. About how dangerous and unnecessary it was. Because"—she glared pointedly at Locke—"if I needed money that badly, he was more than willing to help me out."

"That's not what I did," Locke objected staunchly. "I was offering money to Caroline, not you. And part of my motive was to allow you to keep representing dangerous, crazy clients."

"True."

"So? Are you still in love with him?"

She stared in amazement. "I never was. How could I love a hypocrite like that? I was just grateful he showed his true colors before it really got serious. And once I cooled down, I realized it was my own fault. I chose him because he was a protector by nature—a protector of society, that is—and then I resented it when he wanted to protect *me*. But he was also a liar, because he pretended to be okay with my career when he really wasn't. He lied to me and to himself, because he never really wanted a girl like me."

Locke cleared his throat. "Was it Pete Hanover?"

"What?" Josie laughed in delight. "Hardly. He caved on the second date, when all I did was talk about representing a sixteen-year-old drug dealer. Pete Hanover," she added firmly, "was very upfront about looking for someone to protect. He found her."

"And you're looking for a cop who doesn't want to keep you safe? That's unrealistic, Josie."

"Some of the really strong movie heroes do it." She smiled. "Sean Connery, Mel Gibson, Kurt Russell—they can save the day without reducing their women to victim status."

"Heroes? They're just actors," Locke scoffed. "I'll bet none of them even knows how to load a gun, much less save the day with it. Plus, I'm sure I've seen Sean Connery save helpless heroines, tons of times."

"Maybe so. I guess I'm willing to make an exception for him. Let me know when *you* get that sexy."

"Let me know when *you* get less obnoxious. In the meantime"—he smiled apologetically—"I've got to get back to work. Can we continue the argument later?"

"It's a date." Josie sighed as he returned to studying the maps Isaac had faxed to him at the airstrip. The sites of all the big fireworks displays planned for the area in which the arsonist usually struck were now circled in red. Most of the celebrations were scheduled on the Fourth, but half a dozen would take place that very evening, and Locke wanted to be ready for anything.

And as much as Josie wanted the investigation to heat up, she secretly hoped the bad guy would wait until the Fourth to pull his stunt. Because the incendiary display that currently caught her imagination most was the one she knew could light up her life that very evening if she and Locke were able to finally be alone in a completely private bed.

Isaac Greene had the best smile Josie had ever seen. Warm and sexy, as was the twinkle in his dark amber eyes. Locke had given her some of the less visceral but equally charming details, like the fact that Isaac had been married to, and madly in love with, the same woman for almost twenty years. Isaac was a more experienced agent than Locke, having been with the Bureau for almost a decade longer, but they functioned strictly as equals, and clearly had unlimited respect for each other's skills as well as for their hunches. Needless to say, they were also best friends.

Isaac had picked them up at a small suburban airport, greeting Josie with a playful whistle and the observation that "I see my partner wasn't exaggerating about you."

Josie had voiced surprise that Locke had even mentioned her, to which Isaac had responded, "Mentioned? Warned is more like it."

Now they were seated in a dark booth in the back of a bustling steak house, where the two men were methodically going over plans for deployment of teams for the evening's surveillance. Locke's arm was draped casually over Josie's shoulders, and it felt exactly right, as though they were suddenly the perfect couple! Locke was strong and smart and sexy and fun—and best of all, she had finally found a cop who was willing to actually escort her *into* danger for a change.

They didn't exclude Josie from the conversation, but she tried to sit quietly and listen as much as possible, knowing that bringing along a nosy girlfriend was probably not standard Bureau protocol. Why else were they meeting here rather than at some official headquarters?

Still, when Jessica's name popped up, Josie couldn't help but ask as casually as possible, "Is she coming to L.A. for this operation?"

"The Amazon?" Isaac grinned. "Nah, she doesn't think much of Locke's theory to start with, so the false-gods thing leaves her cold. Of course"—he winked toward his partner—"everything leaves Jessica cold."

Josie grimaced at the use of the word "Amazon." How much had Locke told this guy anyway?

"Don't worry though," Isaac teased. "I stuck up for you. And I told her to follow up on your other idea too."

"My other idea?" Josie flushed. "What was that?"

"I asked her to run a check on all kids arrested ten or twelve years ago in the Chicago area for setting bowls of cereal on fire."

The two men burst into laughter, and Josie sent Locke what she hoped was a withering glare. "No wonder you can't catch this guy. Try to focus, will you?"

"Right now I want to focus on getting you settled in at my place." Locke smiled. "Have you had enough cops and robbers for one afternoon? I think Isaac has things under control for now."

She bit her lip as two competing urges struggled for dominance. She wanted to be alone with Locke, but she didn't want to be a distraction to him. And she *definitely* didn't want to miss anything. Isaac was sweet and clearly competent, but he seemed like the type who might try to handle a call on his own in order to allow his partner to pursue other, more romantic interests. They hadn't come all this way just to be left out of the main event!

Locke seemed to be reading her mind. "Let me rephrase that: Your involvement in this phase is officially over. I've lived up to my part of the bargain. Now I want to dump you at my place so I can help Isaac." Before she could protest, he added more gently, "Maybe tonight I can take you on a tour of the other crime scenes, while we're waiting to hear something. How's that?"

"Will you let me wear one of those FBI windbreakers with the big yellow letters on the back?"

"We'll see." He turned to his partner. "Drop us off at my place and give me a couple of hours to get her settled in. Then I'll meet up with you downtown to finalize things."

"A couple of hours?" Isaac teased. "Just how settled are you two gonna get? Never mind, I don't think I want to know." His tone grew brisk. "Just enjoy yourselves. If anything breaks, I'll be sure to let you know."

Josie felt almost shy as Isaac's car sped toward Locke's condominium, and she was glad she was in the backseat, where she could more easily collect her thoughts. Things were suddenly moving too quickly, away from cops-and-robbers, but into an equally dangerous and unpredictable arena. Until then, there had been so many obstacles to their intimacy. Peeping grandmas, dead heroes, sandstorms. What would happen when all these restraints were removed?

She was so wrapped up in her thoughts that she didn't even try to eavesdrop on the agents' last minute planning session. Even when an occasional round of salutes or other firecrackers split the dusky evening, Josie didn't flinch. And when Isaac's cellular phone rang and the two men in the front seat stopped conversing, it barely registered in the backseat. Then Isaac made a sharp U-turn in the middle of a busy street, and Locke turned in his seat to look at Josie with an expression filled with so much frustration and excitement that she instinctively knew this was it. Even before a siren wailed in the distance, she knew.

"There's a fire?" she demanded. "This early? Do you think it's him?"

"Listen carefully," Locke growled. "We're going to drop you off—"

"Don't you dare! There's no time, and *I want to be there*. I'll stay in the car—"

"Dammit, Josie!"

"If she stays in the car, she'll be fine," Isaac interrupted. "Dropping her off in this neighborhood is more dangerous than bringing her with us." He fixed a stern stare on her reflection in the rearview mirror. "You give us any grief, and I swear I'll tie you up and gag you myself."

"I'll be good," Josie promised gleefully. "I've done this a million times."

The two men debated briefly, but it seemed Isaac had been correct. There was simply nothing to do with Josie short of taking her along with them.

Three minutes of harrowing, wheel-screeching excitement ensued, and then they were there.

A small crowd had gathered in front of a boarded up auto repair shop to watch as firemen extinguished a small blaze in an abandoned rusted-out truck. Was this the work of a restless juvenile? A disgruntled insurance-seeking owner? It didn't seem likely, from all Josie had learned, that this was Locke's arsonist. The man had never targeted a car, and there didn't appear to be a church spire in sight.

Isaac pulled up along a curb half a block away. "You can sit up here in my seat, Josie. That way you can have a better view. I'll lock you in—safe and sound— and you'll stay put. Right?"

Locke studied her warily. "This doesn't look like our guy, but Isaac and I want to take a look around. Alone."

Josie smiled sweetly. There was really no point in testing them, when this was so clearly a false alarm. Better to demonstrate complete compliance so they'd be more likely to bring her along on the next alert. "You're the boss."

"Don't forget it." He helped her out of the backseat and motioned toward the driver's door. "In you go."

She started to obey, but when Isaac moved to the trunk and pulled out bulletproof vests and the coveted FBI jackets, she weakened. They were going to have so much fun without her! "If we don't think this is the arsonist anyway, what harm can it do for me to tag along?"

"I knew it." Locke shook his head in disgust. "Just do what you want, then. But first hand me Isaac's keys, will you?"

Josie kissed his cheek. "No wonder they call you Special. Thanks, Locke." She slipped into the driver's seat and felt for the keys. "They don't seem to be here."

Locke grinned a dark, angry grin, then reached for her arm. Before she could react, he had snapped a handcuff on her wrist and had secured her tightly to the steering wheel. "We'll be right back."

"Locke Harper!" she wailed as he slammed the door in her startled face. "Are you crazy? I'll sue you for this!"

Isaac's roar of laughter completed her humiliation, and she almost didn't twist in her seat to watch as the partners donned their equipment and their windbreakers.

"Jackasses!" She forced herself to take a deep breath as the two men strode toward the fire without bothering to even glance at their prisoner. They were so full of themselves! Typical macho studs, convinced they had overpowered a poor little female for her own good.

"There's only one little problem with that particular fantasy," she informed them as she reached her free arm over the seat and located her bulging purse. "I may not have a black belt in karate, but I have something that works just as well in situations like this. Better, even. Now, where *is* it?" She rummaged through layers of papers, coin purses, compacts, and pens until she finally located her key ring.

The handcuff key had been a gag gift from Pete Hanover, but Josie had instinctively known it would come in handy one day. Now, as she freed herself, she simultaneously plotted Locke's downfall. For one thing, she was not going to let him "settle her in" at his condominium, tonight or ever. More important, she was going to conduct her *own* hunt for the arsonist. After all, the fireworks-as-false-gods theory was hers! She was the one who knew it best. By excluding her, Locke and Isaac were making the biggest mistakes of their careers.

She had seen how Isaac opened the trunk of his sedan by means of a lever under the steering wheel, and so she pulled it before she grabbed her purse and exited the vehicle. If there was any justice in the universe, there'd be one of those stupid windbreakers left for her!

And there was. The jacket, complete with huge yellow lettering; another bulletproof vest; assorted flashlights; and even a rifle. "Too bad I'm not one of those sharpshooting Amazons," Josie mocked. Still, the flashlight would come in handy, and the windbreaker, while ten sizes too big, was everything she'd hoped it would be. Slipping into it, she remembered a canister of Mace—another gift from Peter—that was hopefully somewhere in her purse. In the right hands, namely Josie's, it would be as effective a weapon as the rifle would be in Jessica's.

This time she didn't bother to rummage. Instead, she dumped the contents of her purse into Isaac's trunk and easily located the Mace canister. As she was scooping everything back into her huge leather shoulder bag, she heard a single footstep behind her, and she groaned in frustration, certain it was Locke, and doubly certain he had plans to ruin her fun again. He'd probably even arrest her for impersonating a federal agent!

Resisting an impulse to spin around and glare, she didn't see the person who dealt a single sharp blow to the back of her head, sending her into a spiral of mind-numbing, consciousness-stealing pain.

In what Josie fervently hoped was a dream, huge chunks from the ceiling of the Greybill mansion were crashing down around her, burying her, while clouds of dust stung her eyes and caused her temples to throb. Greybill himself was shouting obscenities, calling her "cottage trash" and pelting her with diamonds and rubies. He seemed to think she was Caroline Galloway, and for some reason believed not only that she had killed him, but that she was a greedy ingrate who had seduced him for the purpose of stealing his precious jewelry collection. Josie wanted to defend herself, but she couldn't speak, or move her arms or legs, or even take a real breath. She was the ultimate helpless victim, and she couldn't help but wonder where Locke Harper and all the other jackasses were now that she actually needed to be rescued!

Then her head began to clear, enough so that she could see she wasn't in the mansion at all. Instead, she was in a dimly lit, eerily silent meeting place of some sort. She still couldn't move her arms, but not because she was buried.

She was handcuffed to a bench rail. And gagged for good measure. For some reason, it made her think of Isaac Greene. But the man who stood before her, studying her as though she were his science project, was Isaac's opposite in every respect—small and fragile, with luminous blue eyes and thin, colorless lips. And, Josie noted wryly, between eighteen and twenty-seven years of age.

Her purse was on the bench beside her, although just out of reach. And she was still wearing all her clothes, including the windbreaker. That was a good sign, she decided groggily. At least this man hadn't molested her thus far. Other than trying to crack her skull, of course.

"Good. You're awake. I didn't want you to miss the show."

Josie tried to swallow, but her mouth and throat had long since dried out. And the gag in her mouth wasn't helping. Not that she wanted to talk to this psycho. Not yet anyway. Not until she knew what buttons *not* to push.

"I'll take that thing out of your mouth if you promise not to scream. If you decide to scream anyway, I'll Mace you."

Josie mentally kicked herself for arming him, then nodded submissively. When he'd freed her mouth, she managed to croak, "You should get out of here. The FBI will find you."

"The FBI?" he taunted. "Isn't that *you?* Or do your initials just happen to match theirs?"

"My initials?" She kicked herself again. "I'm not a federal agent. I'm a criminal defense attorney. I can help you if you just trust me."

"A lawyer?" His blue eyes cooled. "I hate lawyers."

Perfect, Josie groaned inwardly. "You still need to be sensible. Until now you haven't hurt anybody. The FBI respects that about you, and so do I." She smiled with carefully feigned sympathy. "My name's Josie. What's yours?"

"It's Bill. *Not* Billy."

Josie's vision had come back into focus, and she could see now that they weren't in a meeting hall after all. They were in a church. Not *near* a church, but *in* one. And either the cleaning staff left something to be desired, or the arsonist had plans for the place, because right in the middle of the center aisle was a pile of rags, vestments, and other assorted kindling, just waiting to be lit.

Locke will figure it out, she assured herself. *In the meantime, keep him talking.* "Did you set the fire in that old truck?"

He shook his head. "Some amateur. But I was nearby, so I thought I'd check it out. That's when I saw you, getting ready to come after me. To put an end to my ministry. I couldn't believe you knew I'd be there! So I had to stuff you into my car and bring you here with me." He cocked his head and studied her. "I thought it was the big guy with the black hair who was dogging me. Are you his partner or something?"

"I told you, I'm not FBI. I defend criminals in court. I'm pretty good at it too. And I can tell you that you've got a workable defense right now, but if you accidentally kill me—"

"Accidentally?" The arsonist laughed roughly. "I never do anything by accident." Stepping closer, he murmured, "You remind me of my sister. She was always telling me what to do."

"It's my job to advise criminals—"

"I'm not a criminal!" He composed himself rapidly. "The work I do is sacred. Do you think I care whether some lawyer or cop or whatever you are thinks? Your partner understands it better than you, at least. I saw his face once, when he was looking at the fire, and I think he got it."

"He did," Josie assured him nervously. "He'll be surprised, though, to see that you're setting fires *inside* the churches now. Doesn't that glorify the church? People will stand outside and watch it in flames and think it looks holy."

"They're too stupid to understand what I do. I do it for myself. And I *don't* have to explain myself to you."

"Okay, okay." Josie shrugged. "Go ahead, then. Light the fire. I'll witness it for you, or whatever."

"And then you'll identify me to the police?" He shook his head. "I have a better idea."

Josie struggled to keep her growing panic from showing on her face. "If you kill me, I won't see the fire."

"See it?" He laughed. "If I do this right, you'll *be* it."

As she watched in confused horror, he reached into a tattered knapsack and pulled out a thick gray package, which he threw onto the pile of tinder. "Explosives," he explained. "To speed things up. It should be quite a show. And"—his tone was almost sincere—"it's an honor for you, you know. You'll be the first martyr to our holy cause."

Just go! Josie ordered him silently. *Run like the coward you are. Then I can get my handcuff key and be right behind you.* Aloud, she was more diplomatic. "The FBI will be here any minute. Unless *you* want to be the first martyr to your holy cause, I suggest you get going. Don't worry about me," she added sarcastically. "I'll be fine."

She immediately regretted the quip. The arsonist's face contorted with anger, and she realized that his ego was too fragile at moments like this to take any kind of disrespect. "My sister laughed at me," he warned her between clenched teeth.

"I'm just scared. Because I'm scared to death of fire. It's not about you, Bill. I promise."

The explanation seemed to relax him. "We fear things we don't understand. But you'll understand once you're part of the flame. I even envy you. You don't deserve it. But . . ." He pulled a lighter from his pocket, flicked it expertly, and, when a small flame appeared, threw it onto the pile of fodder.

To Josie's amazement, the man's entire demeanor changed at that moment, and she knew for a fact that it was he who was deathly afraid. Not of her or of being caught, but of the fire. The small, almost laughable fire that was starting in one corner of the heap, a full foot from the packaged explosive. She remembered something Locke had told her from the profile. That the arsonist had probably been burned, but not badly, early in life. Enough to scar him mentally but not enough to leave a usable record in any hospital.

Still, he didn't run, although he clearly wanted to do just that. He was looking frantically, from the fire to Josie and back again, as though he suddenly didn't quite know what to do. But Josie knew what she needed, and that was for him to run, so that she could get her purse, find the key, and free herself!

"Go! They'll be here any minute. It's too late to change your mind."

He gave her an almost grateful glance, then turned and sprinted for the door.

There was no time for subtlety or grace as Josie contorted herself until her leg was on the bench. Then she maneuvered clumsily until the purse strap was hooked over her foot. It wasn't going as smoothly as she'd hoped, and she didn't have the guts to look at the bonfire to see how much time she had left, but still she refused to panic. There would be time for falling apart later. First, she had to save herself. *Just get the key, Josie. You can do it. . . .*

Wriggling until the purse was just under her hand, she began to finger the contents carefully, thrilled that her crazy plan was actually going to work.

"Josie!"

A pair of strong arms enveloped her against an equally strong chest.

"What? Oh, good grief!" She felt herself exhale— really exhale!—for the first time in an hour. "Locke! He put some kind of explosive in that pile."

"Dang!" Pulling a key ring from his pants pocket, Locke freed Josie from the cuff, then threw her over his shoulder and bolted for the doorway.

The explosion came just as they cleared the threshold, shattering the silence with an unearthly roar, then splitting the night with a blaze of hot white light. The sheer force of the blast sent Locke and Josie flying to the pavement, where he tried his best to shield her as they were pelted by a storm of flying glass and debris.

"Josie? Are you okay? I can't believe I let him get his hands on you," Locke insisted mournfully.

"*You* didn't let him. I did it all myself. And I was handling it just fine!" She squirmed until she was out from under him, then stared at him in complete frustration. "Are you happy now?"

"Huh?"

Josie could actually feel tears of disappointment sting her eyes. "I was handling it just fine. I had the purse, and I would have been free in five seconds, but no! You *had* to rescue me, right?" Struggling to her feet, she stared at the flaming church, wondering if Locke could possibly understand how pivotal the moment had been to their relationship.

He had rescued her, even though she hadn't needed it. Part of her knew she had no right to complain about that. What was he supposed to have done? Stand outside the church and hope for the best while she roasted?

He had done the only thing a guy like him could do in a situation like that. She couldn't fault him. He was a hero. And she was the helpless victim. It was all too perfect, and all too unfair, for words.

For the first time, she saw that there were others present. Firemen battling the flames. And Isaac frisking Bill. And gawkers. Too many gawkers.

And in the distance, sirens wailing. The ambulance and more fire trucks and more cops. All to rescue Josie.

Once their wounds had been treated and Josie had given a brief statement and a positive identification, Locke escorted her to his condo in silence. She wasn't sure if he was angry or wary or simply tired of the whole mess. As usual, she could gain no clue from his expression. Her own feelings were a jumble too, but one thing was clear. It was a moment they should have been celebrating. Instead, they were as distant as strangers.

He didn't really speak until they reached the elevator. "Are you still mad?"

"I never was. I just thought there was more to us than the big, strong hero and the helpless little victim. Plus"—her voice cracked with frustration—"I had it under control. Really."

He studied her soberly. "It didn't even occur to me to let you handle it on your own, but I have to be honest. Even if I'd thought of it, I still wouldn't have taken the chance. It's my job, Josie."

She smiled sadly. "You're good at it. And I'm a total ingrate. Don't think I don't know it. I haven't thanked you for risking your life—"

"It's okay." The elevator came to rest at the seventh floor, and he led her into the hall, then stopped her with soft restraint. "I have to get back, you know. Once I get you . . . well, settled in . . . I need to do some paperwork and talk to the suspect."

"His name's Bill. Read him his rights," Josie teased halfheartedly.

"No problem."

"I'll be okay, Locke. Just point me toward the shower, and I'll be fine."

He unlocked the door and ushered her into his living room.

"This is nice," Josie murmured, taking in the soft gray and white tones listlessly. "I'll be fine."

"So you said." He turned her toward himself and insisted awkwardly, "At the risk of making a complete fool of myself, there's something I'd like to say."

"As your attorney, I'd advise against it."

Locke's smile faded. "This has to be said. For the record, if nothing else."

"Okay, shoot."

"Can we sit?" He urged her gently toward an over-sized smoke-colored sofa.

Josie's heart ached for him at that moment. She knew, because of her own distress, that he was feeling their relationship slip away. They were clearly so perfect for each other on a physical and playful level. And their mutual respect was beyond question. It was so unfair that they had been forced to confront the obvious—that he was a protector in search of a victim and she was unwilling to be cast in that role, even for the man of her dreams.

He slipped his arm around her shoulder. "I know what you think. That I enjoyed rescuing you. It's not true, Josie."

"Maybe 'enjoyed' is the wrong word," she agreed. "Let's say you *needed* to rescue me."

"Don't you want to know why?"

She shrugged. "Isn't it obvious? You're very brave—"

"Brave?" He laughed harshly. "Desperate is more like it."

"Hmm?"

"You almost had me convinced, you know. Between

the stuff about Grandfather and Caroline and the hokey advice from your love life and all that, I almost believed I really was looking for a victim who would cling to me. But it isn't true, and I can prove it."

Josie flushed under his ardent stare. "How?"

"Remember when I hypnotized you? When you were completely under my power? You were passive and vulnerable and so incredibly submissive and beautiful that you took my breath away."

Josie leaned against him and sighed. "This isn't helping, you know. It's flattering, but it isn't helping."

"Pay attention. You were completely helpless. And I loved it. For about forty-five seconds. Then I got impatient. I started missing you. The *real* you. The pain in the ass, who can take care of herself, and take care of her grandmother, and take care of her clients—without any help from me. The Josie who could keep me in line, and make me feel great about myself, and drive me insane with her constant badgering."

Josie was beginning to tingle all over. "Go on."

"Passive, helpless Josie was pretty, but she was also boring as hell. I wanted *my* Josie back. The obnoxious one."

"Me?" She blushed in confused delight. "That's so sweet, Locke. If I thought it was true . . ." She stared hopefully into his eyes. "I could have saved myself, you know."

"I have no doubt," he assured her huskily. "But I couldn't take that chance. I had plans for you. For *us.* I don't want to be your hero, Josie Galloway. I just want to be your lover."

"Well, then . . ." She stroked his cheek and smiled tentatively. "What on earth are you waiting for?"

TEN

"Interesting dilemma," Locke murmured, catching her hand in his own and kissing it lightly.

Josie knew exactly what he meant. As a dedicated professional, he was dying to get back to work so that he could be a part of wrapping up the most challenging case of his career thus far. But he was also sorely tempted to abandon himself to this, their first real chance to make love with absolute privacy.

"You should go and do your job," she instructed him fondly. "I'll be here—showered, rested, and naked—when you get back."

"That sounds promising. Except for one last detail."

"Oh?"

He cleared his throat before explaining. "We've been so busy discussing the rescue, we didn't deal with the other incident."

"There was another incident?"

"I handcuffed you to the steering wheel. Out of concern for your welfare, but still . . ." He grimaced as though he were mentally kicking himself. "You were pretty mad at the time."

She had forgotten all about that "incident," and was pleased to hear he'd been feeling suitably guilty over it. "Just apologize nicely, and we'll forget it ever happened."

"No problem." He smiled in relief. "In retrospect, I can see it was a mistake. If Isaac and I had taken you with us in the first place, Billy Cole would never have gotten his hands on you. In that sense, it was all my fault."

"That's your apology?" She shook her head in amused disbelief. "You're officially hopeless, Agent Harper. Go interrogate your prisoner."

"Are you still going to be naked when I get back?"

"That depends." She lay back so that her head rested on the arm of the sofa. "Come here and give me some incentive."

Locke stretched out over her, slipping one hand under her back and the other behind her head. Then he lowered his mouth to hers, kissing her more gently than he'd ever done before but every bit as thoroughly.

"Mmm . . ." Josie sighed. "Can't Isaac handle things alone?" Before Locke could answer, she added huskily, "You'd better get out of here while you still can."

"I'm crazy about you, you know." His lips tasted hers again, then his grip tightened and he nuzzled her longingly. "I want to give you my full attention, Josie. It's not like the case is more important—"

"I'll enjoy it more if I get some sleep first."

His smile was sheepish but grateful. "I'll be back in three hours. Tops." Rolling to his feet, he flashed one last tortured grin, then ambled toward the door, where he turned to study her one last time. "There's soda in the fridge. And microwave dinners in the freezer. Help yourself." His blue eyes narrowed slightly. "You're not gonna go out anywhere, are you?"

"Where would I go?" she teased, then she added reassuringly, "Once I call and check on Grandma, I'll shower and hop into bed. I promise. You can lock me in if you want."

"Like that would hold you?" He laughed at the fruitlessness of the concept. "Just stay put this time. I'll be back before you know it. Feel free to snoop around."

She watched him disappear and smiled when she heard the unmistakable click of a dead bolt. The rescue notwithstanding, he really was quite a guy. Her grandmother had picked a winner this time, and the least the granddaughter could do was thank her.

She had left her cellular phone with Caroline, instructing her to leave the power on. Still, it didn't surprise her when she reached her voice mail service instead. She hated to settle for leaving a message but apparently had no choice. "Good grief, Grandma, I told you to just leave the phone turned on. It hardly uses any battery power. Anyway, if you check for messages, call me back at Locke's apartment. I left the number on the counter. And don't worry. Locke caught the arsonist and we're both still in one piece. We'll be back tomorrow with all the details. It's a great story.

"I hope you're not too lonely, sweetie. I love you to death. Sleep tight, okay?"

Locke had given her permission to "snoop," and so she poked around enough to confirm that his condo was a typical bachelor pad *and* to be certain that no female was keeping any belongings in his nightstand or medicine cabinet. Then she turned the shower water on full force, basking in the steamy luxury while washing away the last remnants of the explosion at the church. Except for a few deep scrapes and bruises on her elbows and forearms, and the weariness that was beginning to settle into her joints, she had apparently emerged unscathed from the adventure.

As she towel-dried her wavy hair in front of the bathroom mirror, she longed for access to some makeup or at least some moisturizer. But everything had been in her purse, which had gone up in flames hours earlier. And even if she and Locke had remembered to bring her suitcase up from the car, she couldn't have used anything in it, since the suitcase key had been on the same ring as the handcuff key and had suffered the same pulverizing fate. Eventually, she would find a locksmith for the suitcase and replace her credit cards and license, but for now she was content to simply commandeer one of Locke's flannel pajama tops, rinse and hang her lingerie, and throw her jeans into his washing machine. Then she climbed into his king-size bed, snuggled into the pillows, and was sleeping almost instantly.

* * *

"Josie?"

"Mmm, I missed you." She cuddled against him in the dark, pleased by the hard feel of his muscles and charmed by the strains of a love song playing in the background. He had thought of everything. Well, almost everything. Drawing her toe along his jeaned leg, she complained, "Why are you still dressed?"

"I didn't want to be presumptuous. So? We're still . . . ?"

"Definitely."

His hand immediately slid up her thigh and over her bare backside. "Nice."

"I borrowed one of your shirts."

"Yeah, I noticed." He drew her against himself and murmured, "At the risk of being called a jackass, I have a request."

Josie laughed in charmed delight. "What can I do for you?"

"It occurred to me that we've danced together every night since we met. So I thought . . ."

"That's why you put the music on?"

"Yeah. Plus, I didn't want the neighbors to hear it when you scream out my name."

"Promises, promises." She pulled free enough to stare into his lean, handsome face. "I'd love to dance with you. Tonight and every night for . . . well, for the rest of the week."

"And every night after that," he assured her solemnly. Then he scooped her up, held her for a long, ardent moment, and set her on her feet on the floor. His hands rested on her hips while hers slipped behind his neck. Then he pulled her against him, and they began to sway to the beat of a fifties love ballad.

"You smell great."

"Shampoo and soap," she sighed. "I planned this a little differently, but all in all I wouldn't change a thing." She worked open a button on his shirtfront and slipped her hand inside, stroking his smooth, muscled chest admiringly. "Dancing was a good idea."

"Yeah."

"Did Bill wait for his attorney? Or did he spill his guts the minute Special Agent Locke Harper walked into the interrogation room?"

"How'd you know?"

"He admired you. Plus, he felt some kind of kindred spirit with you because you appreciated the spirituality of the flames."

"Yeah, so he said." Locke nibbled her ear gently, then moved his mouth to her neck.

"Did Jessica congratulate you and Isaac?"

"Not in this lifetime," he murmured as he nuzzled her.

"Is he going to have a public defender or private counsel?"

"P.D."

Josie smiled. "Maybe tomorrow, when you're not in heat, you can give me some more details."

"Sure." Locke slid his hands down her backside until they were cupping her buttocks. "Remind me."

"Mmm." Josie moved against him with slow, greedy interest, then laced her fingers in his dark hair and pulled his mouth down to her own. He seemed to have been waiting for this signal that their stilted conversation was officially over and proceeded to plunge his tongue into her mouth. They practically inhaled each other until neither had enough oxygen to continue, then she pulled her mouth free and tilted her head back, knowing he'd now target her throat with his kisses.

She loved the short, ragged, shallow breaths he was taking, recognizing they were the sounds of a man who was almost out of control with pent-up arousal. She didn't want to give him a chance to recover, and so she quickly unfastened the rest of his shirt buttons and spread it open, covering the taut, hard surface of his chest with playful nips and kisses. Then she unbuckled his belt and unhooked the top button of his jeans. Raising her eyes to his for permission to continue, she flushed at the feverish approval she saw there. Then he took his hands from her and began to remove his shirt, and she kissed his chest again, then trailed kisses down his torso until she was kneeling before him. Unzipping his jeans, she tugged them, along with his briefs, down his powerful thighs.

His erection was a magnificent magnet for her lips and tongue, yet she had barely begun to lick and tease, when he reached down and pulled her, in one smooth motion, up and into his arms. "In bed," he explained hoarsely. Then he lifted her and deposited her on top of the covers while simultaneously stepping out of his clothing.

She stared with heightened, almost giddy delight at his tanned, naked form. Suddenly, she was the one who was overdressed, but Locke didn't seem to mind.

Instructing her gruffly to "Lie back and relax," he put his huge hands between her thighs and forced them gently apart before lowering his mouth to savor the moistness.

She wanted to protest that this was all out of sequence for her! She wanted more kissing and some plain old face-to-face coupling first. Then his tongue probed her expertly and she realized with a sharp, grateful gasp that he knew exactly what he was doing. Instinctively wrapping her legs around his neck, she luxuriated in his plundering until the sensations of pleasure became so focused and wrenching that she arched into him, calling his name softly just as the moment of complete ecstasy gripped her.

His mouth stayed to comfort her for a long, soothing moment before he extracted himself from her legs and crawled up to lie beside her, wiping the back of his hand across his mouth with exaggerated satisfaction, as though he'd just indulged in a succulent, extravagant banquet.

She curled her arms around his neck. "Give me a kiss."

He obliged gently, then complained, "Are you ever going to get naked like you promised?"

She laughed and began to unbutton her shirt, but he had a faster solution, pulling the still-fastened garment over her head and throwing it aside. As he studied her full breasts and erect nipples, his cobalt eyes seemed to blaze with admiration, but all he said was, "Nice."

"You can touch them if you want."

He chuckled and bent his head down over her

chest, nipping appreciatively at the rosy, hardened peaks, thrilling Josie easily. Then he was kissing her mouth again while he moved against her rhythmically with his hard, neglected erection.

"Locke?"

"Yeah?"

She reached down to stroke him. "Let's make love."

"Isn't that what we've been doing?"

Moving her mouth to his ear, she admitted, "I want to feel you inside me."

"It's about time." Rolling her onto her back, he stretched his lean form over hers, kissed her mouth with passionate thoroughness, then reached to open the drawer of his nightstand. Locating a flat, silvery packet, he proceeded to rip it open with his teeth.

"Let me," Josie insisted. Taking the condom from him, she knelt beside him and rolled it slowly, firmly, and enticingly over him. Her intention was to prolong every moment of exquisite agony, but she had barely finished when he unceremoniously flipped her onto her back again and urged her thighs apart.

Josie sighed with delight as his fingers indulged in some last-minute courtship, then she locked gazes with him and reached out to guide and stroke until he began to thrust himself into her, gently but insistently.

Her only thought was to satisfy him as completely as he'd done for her, and so she murmured erotic encouragement in his ear while gyrating provocatively. He seemed to love it, groaning with undisguised appreciation while slowing his movements as though determined not to become too stimulated too quickly. He clearly wanted it to last forever, and Josie almost thought it might. Each movement generously fueled the next, building without cresting, arousing without frustrating, and provoking without challenging. Josie marveled at the thought that they'd somehow discovered the secret to eternal, unselfish lovemaking.

Then without warning her less-patient appetites dared to begin clamoring for attention again. Apparently, where Locke was concerned, she was insatiable!

And somehow he knew, because a deep, teasing chuckle was rumbling through his chest. "Aren't you ever satisfied?"

"You're good at this," she moaned in defense. "It's not my fault. Oh!" She began to grind more insistently. "Oh, Locke . . ."

"I know," he growled. Then his thrusts grew rapid and powerful, searing her with pleasure until she shrieked his name just as he groaned in abject, appreciative release.

They clung to one another, entangled and exhausted, until Josie finally broke the silence with a reverent "Wow."

"Yeah, wow." His grin was predictably sheepish. "I knew it would be good, but this . . ."

"I know." She kissed him, then snuggled happily against his chest. "Now I really know why they call you 'special.' "

He pulled a fluffy gray comforter up from the foot of the bed, covering both their forms. "Did you want to get some sleep? Or are you hungry? I could order pizza."

"Pepperoni?"

"Sure. Whatever you want."

Josie tousled his hair. "There's no way I can sleep after that, but then again, I had a nap. You're probably exhausted."

"I'm wide awake." He caressed her torso with long, warming strokes. "I can't believe we've known each other for only four days. I don't think I've ever felt this comfortable with a girl. Woman, I mean."

"I know. It's practically perfect. All that's missing is pepperoni."

Locke chuckled. "You're a slave driver. I'll be back in a minute. Stay put."

"Are you sure you don't want to handcuff me to the bed?"

"Maybe later." Shrugging out from under the cover, he grabbed a dark blue hooded robe from a nearby hook and headed for the living room.

Instantly lonely for him, Josie scooped up the plaid flannel pajama top and hurried after him.

When he'd finished placing his order, he took a moment to ogle her long, bare legs. "Nice look. You should keep that. I never wear it."

"Thanks."

"Do you want some brandy? Or wine? Or orange juice?"

"Juice sounds great."

She watched as he served her a generous portion in a crystal wine goblet. Then he poured an inch of brandy into a snifter and brought both drinks to the glass-topped dining table. "Do you want to watch TV? Or play cards? Hey, that reminds me. Did you reach Caroline?"

"She didn't have the phone on. But I'm sure she's fine. Right?"

"Absolutely. She's probably been sound asleep for hours. Having nostalgic dreams about your grand-father."

"Or nightmares about yours."

"Cute, Josie. Come here and sit on my lap, and I'll tell you all about Bill Cole. And in the morning," he added reassuringly, "we'll call up to the big house and have one of the desk clerks run down and check on Caroline."

They polished off a medium pizza in record time while Locke shared the details of the wrap-up of the arson investigation, with Josie predictably hanging on his every word. "I knew he'd open up to you. I wish he'd waited for his attorney, but I don't really blame him for trusting you. You radiate integrity, you know."

"That sounds boring."

Wiping her lips with a paper napkin, she scooted back into his lap. "You also radiate sex appeal."

"Yeah?" He arched an eyebrow. "Ready for an-other round?"

"Pardon?"

"You know what I mean. You've been flashing those sexy legs around—"

"I don't have anything else to wear," she pouted,

tugging at the hem of the flannel shirt as though desperate to hide her thighs from view.

"Actually, I brought your suitcase up." He gestured toward the entry way. "I was kinda hoping you brought those slinky pink p.j.'s with you."

Josie nodded. "I brought those and my red dress."

His dark eyes twinkled with anticipation. "Even better. You drove me crazy last night, you know."

"Unfortunately, the key to the suitcase is on my key ring, which was in my purse, which went ka-blooey in the church. So unless you know how to pick a lock, you'll have to wait."

"Keys?" He grinned in relief. "Wait a minute."

Josie watched as he disappeared into the bedroom. Now what? Did he have a set of skeleton keys? Or did the FBI actually teach him to pick locks? She'd been kidding about that, but as long as he didn't wreck the suitcase, which had been a graduation gift from her brother—

"One set of keys," he announced as he came back into view. "I almost forgot about them. Isaac found them in the trunk of his car. So?" His blue eyes sparkled with anticipation. "The dress? Or the slinky p.j.'s? Either one works for me."

Josie stared in quiet disbelief. There was no mistaking the pewter medallion that dangled at the end of her keys. Had they honestly been in the trunk of Isaac's car? They must have fallen out of her purse when she was searching for the can of Mace. Which meant she hadn't had them in the church with her at all . . .

"Do you realize what this means, Locke?"

He was instantly wary. "Give me a hint."

Moistening her lips, she explained, "I thought I had the handcuff key. I thought I could free myself. But the key was in Isaac's trunk. Which means . . ." She took a deep breath, then blurted out, "You really *did* rescue me."

"Come on, Josie. Don't dredge that up again. I don't want to fight."

"You don't understand!" Crossing the room, she threw her arms around his neck. "You saved my life."

"You make it sound like a good thing."

"Of course it is, silly." She brushed her lips along his jawline. "Rescuing me when I didn't need rescuing was annoying. But this is different." As a wave of delayed apprehension swept over her, she tightened her grip and murmured, "There's no way I could have freed myself. If you hadn't found me when you did, I would have been blown to bits. I'm so grateful, Locke."

"Forget about it."

"No. I don't want to. I . . . I kinda like it."

"Huh?"

Molding herself against him, she insisted breathlessly, "You really are a big, strong hero. And I really was a helpless victim. I think I'm starting to understand why this excites you guys so much. It's got definite possibilities. And"—she slid her hand under his robe to caress his chest—"since it's not going to happen too often, we should take advantage of it."

"Let me get this straight," he demanded. "Rescuing you is suddenly a turn-on?"

Josie nodded. "I'm weak with appreciation. And

trembling with admiration. And dripping with gratitude." She took his hand and guided it between her
thighs. "See?"

Locke chuckled proudly. "For a strong, independent woman, you make one helluva damsel in
distress."

"And you make one helluva hero. You'd better kiss
me, Agent Harper."

"No problem." His mouth descended to hers, enjoying her roughly, then he swept her up into his
arms and carried her toward the bedroom to claim
his reward.

Truly exhausted, Josie slept late into the morning
and therefore wasn't at all surprised to find her hero
missing from the bed when she awoke. She stretched
and smiled sheepishly, wondering if his memories of
the night before were as vivid and amazing as her
own. Never had she had a lover like him, and she
had to believe that he, too, had been satisfied beyond
expectation.

Her suitcase had been placed on the floor near the
bed, the key already in the lock, and she took it as a
hint that he still wanted to live out the pink-pajama
fantasy. It sounded like a fun way to start the day, just
as the rescue fantasy had been the perfect way to end
the perfect night.

Snapping open the clasp, she grabbed pink satin
with one hand and her makeup kit with the other,
then dashed for his bathroom to pull herself together. Pinning her hair up out of the way, she took

a quick shower, toweled off vigorously, and then slipped into the provocative pajamas, enjoying the silky feel of the fabric against her skin. Locke would love that feeling too, she knew. Eager to indulge him, she took only a moment to brush her hair and coat her lashes with jet-black mascara before taking a deep breath and venturing back into the master bedroom.

He was there, waiting, but to Josie's dismay his eyes didn't light up even though the outfit clearly registered for a second. He was doing his expressionless, unreadable routine again.

I have got to learn how to do that! Josie insisted silently. Aloud she asked carefully, "Is everything okay?"

"Yeah, everything's fine." He crossed to her and took her into his arms, but when Josie slid her hands behind his neck, he stopped the kiss with an awkward "Everything's fine, like I said. Caroline's fine. But—"

"Oh, no!"

"Don't get upset," he pleaded. "It's not her heart. She hurt her ankle, but she's fine now. And we can be there in a couple of hours tops, so just take a deep breath."

"Her ankle?"

It was Locke who took the deep breath before explaining. "I called the front desk this morning to ask if someone could run over and check on her and tell her to turn your phone on so we could reach her. They told me she fell late yesterday afternoon—"

"Yesterday?"

"They took good care of her. That was clear to me. And she wouldn't let them call us. So they took her to the ER and put a cast on her."

"Did they know about her heart? Did they keep her at the hospital? Where *is* she, Locke? Can I talk to her?"

"Shh." His lips brushed hers. "She didn't want to stay at the hospital, and it sounds like there were no complications, so the hotel staff brought her back to Driftwood. They wanted to move her into one of the rooms at the mansion so they could keep a closer eye on her, but she insisted on sleeping at the cottage, so they gave her a beeper and sent someone every couple of hours. She's fine, Josie."

Pulling free, Josie wandered to the bed, where she sat and buried her face in her hands. "I can't stand it that she was all alone. This is my nightmare, Locke. Grandma all alone and hurt, after all the times she was there for me when I needed her."

"I know." He joined her on the bed, fingering her pink satin collar wistfully. "There's a plane waiting for us. Get dressed while I fix you a cup of coffee, and then we can head out. I'm really sorry, Josie. I didn't anticipate anything like this—"

"It's not your fault. Neither of us could have known this would happen," she assured him. "How *did* it happen?"

"The clerk didn't have the details, but apparently, she tried to use those stupid steps down to the beach. She must have wanted to revisit the spots where she and your grandfather hung out years ago."

"Why didn't she wait for us?" Josie grumbled. "You told her you'd help her with them."

"Going there with *us* wouldn't be quite the same,

right? She was reliving memories of being a young woman. With us, she's a grandmother."

"I suppose." Josie pulled herself together and summoned a tremulous smile. "Did you say something about coffee and a plane?"

ELEVEN

The cab ride to the airport, and the plane trip thereafter, were a blur to Josie, but the half-hour excursion along twisty roads in Locke's rented SUV to reach Driftwood Point seemed positively interminable. She was beginning to wonder just how much guilt one granddaughter could bear. She had been oblivious to her grandmother's heart problems; had drained the poor woman's finances down to nothing; had left her alone with her fragile bones in a strange and treacherous place; and had been too busy having mad, passionate sex to know or care whether the poor woman was lying on a gurney in an emergency room.

"I'm a bad, bad granddaughter."

Locke grinned sympathetically. "Remind me to spank you later."

"Very funny."

"She's fine, Josie. I feel bad that we left her too, but she *wanted* us to go. To be alone together. If you had stayed with her while I went to L.A., you both would have been miserable."

"I suppose."

"I got the impression she liked the idea of being alone," he continued stubbornly as he negotiated a particularly sharp curve in the road. "It wasn't just the matchmaking that made her send us away."

Josie nodded. "Instead of returning to the scene of the crime, she was trying to return to the scene of the honeymoon. I should have expected the rest. I should have made her promise to stay away from those stupid steps. Every time I close my eyes, I see her crumpled in a heap at the bottom."

"Yeah, me too."

She was amused by his tortured tone. "You feel guilty too?"

"Yeah."

"I guess I see your point. You drag a poor old lady off to the beach, then abandon her. That's not exactly heroic behavior."

"True. Then again, she's not *my* grandmother."

"Thanks a lot. Oh, there's the turnoff!" Josie blinked back an unexpected rush of tears. "I *hate* this stupid place."

"Join the club," Locke growled in almost savage agreement. "I say we pack her up, put her in the backseat with her foot elevated, and get the hell out of this dump."

"I can't believe you want to leave." Caroline was protesting moments later as she extricated herself from her granddaughter's clinging arms. "What on earth did the hotel staff tell you? I'm perfectly fine,

Josie. It's sweet of you to be so worried, but I just took a little tumble and twisted my ankle." She reached out to grasp Locke's hand as she added, "I wish you hadn't rushed back on my account."

"Wild horses couldn't have kept me away, Caroline. I'm just sorry we weren't here to take care of you last night."

"The hotel staff has been spoiling me rotten."

"I'm sure they've been great. But you'll be more comfortable at home—"

"Don't be silly!" Caroline scolded. "You aren't listening, Locke. I'm fine. And I have the best news. In fact, I have two pieces of wonderful news."

"Did they give you anything for the pain?"

"Pain?" Caroline scoffed. "I still don't believe it's broken. Now that the swelling's gone down, I think they should X-ray it again. I'm perfectly fine."

He felt a wave of admiration for this woman. For both of the Galloway females, in fact. They seemed to have a limitless capacity to love unselfishly and to make life interesting in the process.

"So what's the big news, Grandma?" Josie demanded as she settled into the overstuffed chair near the bed. "Have they condemned that awful stairway? If they don't, we may have to sue them."

"They've been absolutely wonderful to me," Caroline repeated firmly. "I don't want to hear any talk of lawsuits or such. Of course . . ." Her green eyes began to twinkle. "I may have mentioned you were an attorney. That might be part of the reason they insist that our entire trip is on the house." Beaming toward Locke, she added proudly, "That's the first part of the good news. This trip, meals included, hasn't cost you or the government a dime."

He couldn't help but chuckle. "Nice work, Caroline. What's the second part of the news?"

The grandmother shifted her gaze toward Josie, then back to Locke, before announcing, "We came here to solve the robbery and recover the jewels, and I think I may have discovered the clue that can make that all come true."

Locke was taken by surprise, not because of the announcement per se, but because he had actually forgotten all about the Greybill case. It was as though it had happened in another lifetime. Before he had met Josie. Before he had discovered what truly mattered in life. Not that his grandfather didn't matter anymore, he assured himself hastily. But hadn't his grandfather's legacy been one simple lesson? That a person, particularly a captivating, green-eyed female, was infinitely more important than a case?

Josie didn't seem to share his newfound perspective. Instead, she demanded, "What kind of clue? Did you remember something while you were at the beach? This is perfect, Grandma!"

"I really never made it to the beach," Caroline hedged. "I mean, I fell onto it, and that was the extent of my visit. The clue came from a dream. And the dream, I'm sure, was a direct result of the hypnosis, and so—" She beamed again in Locke's direction. "You should take full credit."

He wondered if they could detect the hint of annoyance he was experiencing. How far was she going to take this ridiculous charade? If it had been anyone else but Josie's grandmother, he might have called her on it. Might have said: *Stop playing games.* But he'd taken advantage of enough Galloway games in the last twenty-four hours to know he had no right to be so judgmental, so he restrained himself, confident that Josie would carry the conversation.

She didn't fail him. "You had a dream, Grandma? About the crime? Don't keep us in suspense! Whodunit?"

"Well, of course I don't know exactly," Caroline sighed. "Dreams can be so vague. All I know is, I heard a woman talking. The same woman I heard when Locke hypnotized me. But this time," the older woman informed them in a hushed, excited tone, "I heard exactly what she said."

Not this again, Locke groaned inwardly.

Josie's reaction was predictably extreme. "What did she say? Do you know her name? Did she have an accomplice? Was she—"

"Josie, please." Caroline held up her hand as though confused by the onslaught of questions. "Just let me tell it exactly as I dreamed it." Turning to Locke, she said quietly, "The woman was clearly well bred. Possibly from the East Coast. I'm not good with accents. But I heard every word she said. She told her companion to take the jewels to the beach and hide them in a crevice in the rocks near the archway. She said to pick a crevice at least seven feet above the sand so that no one could see into it. But to pick one she could easily climb up to later. And here's the best part." Caroline's voice grew rich and confident. "She said they should store the jewels there forever.

That way they could just come back from time to time to take one or two as they needed them, but the rest would stay in the crevice indefinitely. Do you see what that means? There might still be some of the jewels left in the rocks!"

Locke had to take a long look at the cast on Caroline's foot to keep himself from reprimanding her for this foolish lie. How much of this was he expected to tolerate! "That's interesting, Caroline, but my grandfather and his men checked those rocks—"

"You said yourself they missed things," Caroline sniffed.

"That's right," Josie agreed, nudging Locke with her toe as she spoke. "I think it's worth checking out. Don't you, Locke?"

He took Caroline's hand again and explained gently but firmly, "Josie and I have been checking those crevices. If the jewels were there, we would have found them. It was just a dream, Caroline. Let it go. The important thing is you're okay. Don't worry about solving the crime anymore. It just isn't important."

To his chagrin, the older woman's eyes began to fill with tears. It didn't make any sense! He was letting her off the hook. Why was she still making such a big deal of it?

"I'm so embarrassed," she sobbed. "I wouldn't blame you if you hated me after all the trouble I've caused! I thought I could make everything right—"

"You can, Grandma!" Josie sprang toward her grandmother and enveloped her in a bear hug while simultaneously shooting green darts from her eyes in

Locke's direction. "I'm the one who checked the crevices near the archway, and the truth is, I didn't really do a good job. I just eyeballed them from a distance without really getting up close. Locke gave me a hard time about it, in fact. *Remember,* Locke?"

He had the feeling that if he didn't "remember," she would strangle him, or at least never speak to him again, and so, against his better judgment, he said, "Josie's right, Caroline."

"Really?" She dabbed at her eyes cautiously. "Because in the dream it seemed so real."

"Locke checked the ones closer to the cottages, and believe me, he was thorough," Josie explained firmly. "But I didn't use the same system. Now I wish I had. You were right, Locke," she added sweetly. "We'll do it your way from now on."

"You'll check the ones near the archway?" Caroline sighed with relief. "I just know my dream was trying to tell me something."

"We'll check every one," Josie promised. "But you have to accept the possibility that someone else may have removed those jewels later, Grandma. I mean, it's been fifty years, right? Your clue is a great one, but if it doesn't pan out, you have to promise you won't be too disappointed."

Caroline smiled serenely. "I have a feeling those jewels are still there. Call it woman's intuition. But go right away and check. Please? I won't be able to rest until we know for sure."

"That's right, Locke," Josie prompted. "Go and check it out right away."

He knew she could read the disapproval in his eyes,

but he also knew better than to argue. "Sure. Whatever. You're not coming?"

"Of course she is," Caroline interrupted.

"I don't want to leave you alone again, Grandma. Plus, I need to tell you all about the arsonist."

"You can tell me about that later." Caroline pouted. "I thought you'd be more excited, Josie."

"I am. I promise. But I missed you, Grandma. I really can't bear to leave you alone again so soon."

Caroline folded her arms across her chest. "Your place is with Locke at a time like this. He dedicated all his time and resources to solving this robbery. The least you can do is be with him in his moment of glory."

It was too much for Locke, but when he began to protest, Josie literally silenced him, putting her hand over his mouth while she explained grimly, "He doesn't like the idea of leaving you all alone again either, Grandma. How about a compromise? Our hero here can go down ahead of me, and I'll catch up with him once I'm sure you've taken your medications and are sound asleep."

"I suppose that will have to do." Caroline nodded.

Josie's gaze both coaxed and threatened Locke to agree, and so he grumbled, "I'll meet you down there."

"Thanks, Locke. I owe you one."

He had to smile at that, knowing how creatively she could repay a debt. It was almost worth the ridiculous lies and games. In fact, it was absolutely worth it.

* * *

Josie knew she was just postponing the inevitable—
Locke had methodically checked all the likely crevices
near the archway himself!—but the disappointment
in her grandmother's eyes had been too sharp to be
bearable. They needed to find a way to lessen the blow.
To convince her that her failure to help Locke solve
this crime paled in comparison to her success at making the perfect match for a lonely granddaughter.

She also knew that Locke was annoyed with her,
and she couldn't really blame him. He didn't like
"humoring" people any more than he approved of
lying to them. But in this case she was sure he was
being too rigid. Why not let Grandma think her
dream might have been legitimate? Let her believe
that some woman from the East Coast stole the jewels
and hid them near the archway, but they were stolen
again in the interim? Who could that possibly hurt?

In the meantime, she tucked Caroline into bed,
then regaled her with the story of the handcuffs, explosives, and rescue. Caroline was aghast at the news
that Josie had placed herself in jeopardy so blithely,
but she was also thrilled with the news that Josie and
Locke were now officially a couple.

Eventually, the conversation seemed to exhaust the
patient, whose breathing became a relaxed, rhythmic, reassuring snore. Josie stayed for a long while
thereafter, knowing that Locke would understand.
Plus, it never hurt to keep a man waiting, did it? Especially one who could turn impatience into foreplay
so masterfully.

She also needed to give Locke time to forget about
the harmless lie she'd forced on him.

"I'll make it up to him," she vowed as she descended the steep steps to the beach. "I'll promise to be brutally honest from now on. Unless there's a good reason not to be, of course."

She knew he'd be waiting for her near the hut, which by some miracle was still standing. But she could never have predicted the apologetic smile that shone in greeting on his ruggedly handsome face. With a rush of relief she threw her arms around his neck and cooed, "You're the best. And I'm hopeless. Do you forgive me for making you lie?"

He hugged her close, then whispered, "I love you, Josie."

A delicious chill ran up her spine at the unexpected announcement, and she pulled free sharply, needing eye contact more than body contact under the circumstances. "What?"

"I want to keep on seeing you after this vacation is over. I want to dance with you every night. I want to be your hero. And I want to be supportive of your career. You have to believe me when I say that I care about your grandmother. But—"

"Wait!" She put a finger over his lips and insisted, "You just told me you loved me. I don't want there to be a 'but.' " Slipping her hand behind his head, she drew his mouth down to hers for a long, deep, hopeful kiss.

He seemed absolutely engulfed by her, sweeping her up into his arms and into the hut, where they tumbled to the sand, still kissing and murmuring their love for one another. There was a gentle mindlessness to their groping, as though they were no longer on a gloomy beach but were instead in a private paradise of their own making. When Locke had touched every part of her with fevered longing and kissed every part of her with passionate thoroughness, he took her as though life itself depended upon it, and Josie responded in kind, stunned, seduced, and overpowered, all in one electrifying whirlwind. She forgot where they were and who might be walking by and what they might think. All she knew was that she and Locke were the only persons who mattered in this tiny, perfect world of love and sensation. And by some miracle, he seemed to know it too.

And when it was over, he was silent and still, as though the declaration of love, combined with the passionate display, had caught him fundamentally off his guard, leaving him unprepared for the commitment he had now imposed upon himself.

Josie could only imagine the questions that were plaguing him at that moment. Some were logistical—they lived hundreds of miles apart, after all! Was he thinking she'd now show up on his doorstep with bags and grandmother in hand or something? Hadn't this guy ever heard of dating?

Just give him a minute to compose himself, she counseled herself finally. *Go and check the rocks, in case Grandma asks you about it. Which you know she will, so . . .*

"Locke?"

"Yeah?"

"I promised Grandma I'd poke around in the rocks near the archway, so maybe I'll just scoot over there for a few minutes while you . . . well, while you rest. Is that okay?"

"Yeah. That's fine."

The resignation in his tone amused her. Maybe Locke was like her father had once been. What they called a confirmed bachelor. The poor guy had apparently scared himself to death by opening up to a female so completely, especially when he'd known her for only five days. What a jackass!

"Lighten up," she advised coolly as she crawled from the hut. "When I get back, we're going to talk about this, you know."

"Yeah. I know." He leaned up on his elbows. "Hey, Josie?"

"Yes?"

"I meant what I said. I love you. No matter what."

She grinned in relief. "Back off, big fella, and I just might decide to let you take me to the prom." Jumping to her feet, she hurried toward the archway, allowing excitement to bubble in her heart at the thought of *finally* being in love. It was scary—Locke was evidence of that!—but it was also charming and unexpected and utterly perfect. She intended to savor every moment of it.

Then she raised her eyes to the wall of rocks, determined to faithfully scour every nook and cranny for the jewels in spite of the pointlessness of the exercise. Logic dictated that there could be nothing there, because Locke had already checked it thoroughly two days earlier.

Not that Josie was a fan of logic over dreams. She would have loved nothing better than to solve a fifty-year-old crime because of a clue from a dream. And in a way it could still happen, she told herself playfully. It made sense that the hypnosis had stimulated Grandma's memory, causing her to dream about a woman with an eastern accent. Maybe, if they checked Locke's list of suspects, they could identify the voice that had been buried in Caroline Galloway's subconscious for fifty years.

Despite this wishful thinking, a gasp still caught in Josie's throat at the unmistakable sight of a corner of burlap hanging from a crevice in the archway wall. Just about seven feet from the sand. Near the archway. Just where Grandma's dream had told them it would be.

Josie's heart began to pound as she climbed, and when she pulled on the ragged edge of the fabric and found that it was in fact a bundle, she thought she might actually lose her mind with amazement. It took only one solid yank to cause the package to fall from its perch, past Josie's hand and down to the beach below, and when it hit, it broke open, spilling its glorious contents over the otherwise lackluster gray sand.

Emeralds, strung on a delicate gold strand. Diamonds embedded in a substantial silver brooch. Cuff links, earrings, bracelets—all dazzling. All magnificent. All impossible, and yet, all there, at Josie's feet.

Her brain could not keep up with it all. There was the fact that it couldn't be true. The fact that it was almost certainly true. The fact that these jewels were so obviously genuine and priceless. And the fact that somehow, miraculously, they had survived unnoticed for fifty years.

She could buy Grandma a palace with these to replace the home that was in foreclosure! Of course, Locke would never allow that, and neither would Caroline, although she might indulge Josie's fantasy for a while before refusing.

And Josie herself would never really do it, although she wasn't above toying with the idea. These jewels belonged to the Greybills. But the reward belonged to Caroline. And the credit for solving the case belonged to Locke. And Locke belonged to Josie. It was unbelievable!

She couldn't wait to see his face when she told him! He'd be happy and amazed, but also a little peeved, she suspected gleefully. After all, he had searched this very spot, in his maddeningly methodical fashion, and had somehow missed these!

"He must be blind!" She laughed lightly at the frustrated expression she knew she'd soon see. "Even if he missed that particular crevice, how could he miss seeing the burlap when he was searching the part around it? I saw it from a mile away!" Holding a ruby ring up to the overcast sky in a vain attempt to catch a ray of sun, Josie repeated somewhat less enthusiastically, "How did he miss it? He was being so careful."

And then she grudgingly admitted the truth. That he *couldn't* have missed it. Which meant it couldn't have been there. Which meant someone had placed it there *after* Locke's search.

She turned her disbelieving gaze toward Cottage No. 4, but it was just out of sight, and so she sank to the ground and began to gather up the jewels, wrap-

ping them in the burlap without any particular idea
of what she intended to do with them.

Only one thing was certain. She couldn't tell
Locke. Because Locke Harper was not just her friend
and her lover. He was also a federal agent, and as
such he would have no choice but to turn the jewels,
and Caroline Galloway, over to the authorities. He
might even have to testify against her! It would kill
him, and he would plead with them to forgive him,
but just the same, he'd do it. Because he was a "special" agent. A straight-arrow boy scout right out of
the FBI coloring book. Josie had known that from
the start.

And *she* was Caroline Galloway's attorney. But
somehow, when it had mattered most, Josie had stupidly forgotten that.

He was sitting near the water's edge when she returned to the hut, and she forced herself to smile
brightly as she joined him. "I know we said we'd talk,
but I should probably check on Grandma first."

He patted the sand. "Sit with me for a minute."

"Sure." She lounged next to him, poking her toes
into the sand until her feet were half buried. "This
is nice."

"Yeah."

"Aren't you hungry?"

He cupped her chin in his hand. "We need to talk.
No more stalling."

Josie's throat tightened at the thought. How could
she talk to him about their future when they no

longer had one? She couldn't continue to see him and also keep this secret from him. It would eventually tear them apart. And she couldn't tell him. At least, not until she'd gotten the whole story from her grandmother. Maybe by some miracle the obvious would prove to be wrong. Maybe Caroline hadn't hidden the jewels while they were in Los Angeles. Maybe she hadn't pawned two of them. Maybe she hadn't lied to federal agents and to her own granddaughter.

"I have a confession to make, Locke."

His face, of course, was expressionless. What else could she have expected? Even when he nodded for her to continue, she couldn't tell if he expected good news or bad. Little did he know, it was worse than that.

She took a deep breath, desperate not to show how shaky she was at that moment. "I'm absolutely crazy about you. But this relationship has been moving way too fast for me. We need to slow it down. For both our sakes. So I have a huge favor to ask."

"What's that?"

"I want you to get in your car and go back home to L.A. I'll rent something and drive Grandma back to Sutterville tomorrow. You and I will spend a couple of days apart, and then we'll talk."

"I know about the jewels, Josie."

She swallowed but held his gaze. "Jewels?"

She suddenly wished he had continued with his unreadable expression. Anything was better than the hurt she saw now in his face. "You don't trust me? That's incredible to me. After all we've been through—after the way we feel about each other—"

"I'm her lawyer." Josie jutted her chin forward in guarded defiance. "I don't want to discuss it until I've talked to my client." Weakening just a bit, she asked softly, "Why did *you* check the crevices? You knew you'd already scoured that section."

Locke paused, as though needing to choose his words more carefully than ever. "Caroline said the dream was caused by the hypnosis. That it was the same woman she heard and saw then. And I knew she was never hypnotized, so I knew the dream was a lie too."

"She wasn't hypnotized?"

He shook his head.

Josie thought back to the zombielike performance and sighed in belated agreement. "Why didn't you tell me?"

"I actually meant to, but once we were on our way to L.A., I got distracted by the investigation. And then later I got distracted by you." He coughed and added quickly, "I figured she faked the hypnosis because she felt bad about not having any clues for me. And at first I thought the dream was just more of the same. But when I was coming down the steps, I thought about her ankle, and I asked myself what could have been so important that she braved that dangerous stairway. And then I knew. I didn't want to believe it, but . . ."

Josie stared out across the waves. "It's such a mess."

"I can't believe you were actually going to break up with me over it. Don't you see how crazy that was?"

"Are you going to turn my grandmother in?" When he didn't answer right away, she murmured,

"See? I couldn't tell you, Locke. But I also knew I couldn't keep such a big secret from you and still have a strong relationship."

"We'll work it out," he insisted stubbornly.

"How?" Josie shook her head. "Remember when I came down to the beach and you told me you loved me, and wanted to keep seeing me, and cared about grandma, *but* . . . Well, now I know what the 'but' was, and I agree. It's a big one."

"I knew it might get rough." He nodded. "But I figure if we trust each other and work together, we can handle it."

"How? By visiting Grandma in prison together on Sunday afternoons?" Josie mocked.

Locke grasped her by her shoulders and shook her gently. "Cut it out. You're so darned stubborn sometimes. Didn't it ever occur to you that Caroline might not have done it?"

Josie stared in disbelief. "You actually believe that's possible? Are you stupid or something? We *know* the jewels weren't there on Tuesday, we know Grandma came down to the beach on Wednesday. Now suddenly the jewels are here on Thursday? And you think it might be a coincidence?"

Realizing that she had just laid out the prosecution's case for them, she winced as she insisted, "Forget I said any of that."

"She hid the jewels in the rocks," Locke confirmed. "I'm not debating that. I'm just debating whether she stole them in the first place. She could be covering for someone."

"Who? The only person she knew who could

have—*Grandpa*? You're calling my dead grandpa a crook?" Indignation surged through her at the very idea. "First you call my grandmother a liar—"

"Your grandmother *is* a liar," he reminded her coolly. "And your grandfather *is* dead. He can't go to prison, Josie. Isn't that true?"

"He can't go to prison," she repeated slowly.

"And it's likely he's the one who did it, right? I can't picture Caroline overpowering a big man like Greybill, much less masterminding a complex robbery."

"Masterminding?" Josie's stomach knotted. "That's crazy, Locke. You never met him, so you couldn't know, but I spent so much time with him—"

Caroline's words, echoing in her memory, interrupted the stalwart defense. *I learned more about him that week than I'd learned in all the years I'd known him. I saw a side of him that took my breath away.*

"Talk to me, Josie," Locke was insisting. "Trust me."

"I do." She sandwiched his face between her hands. "I trust you completely. I don't know what I was thinking."

"You were thinking I had no choice but to report that we'd located the stolen jewels. And"—he took a deep breath, then admitted quietly—"that's true."

Pulling her into a bear hug, he continued, his voice husky with love and reassurance. "I was worried too, you know. That's what I was going to tell you when you first came down to the beach. That we had to promise each other we wouldn't let this mess come between us, no matter what. I want to help Caroline—"

"I know you do. But . . ." Josie pulled free and smiled apologetically. "I need to talk to her alone first. Please don't be offended—"

"Offended?" He grinned and shook his head. "If I were the type that offended easily, would I still be here?" Rising to his feet, her pulled her gallantly up and into his arms again. "You're her attorney. If she wants to talk to you alone first, no problem. I'll just read her her rights—"

"Locke Harper! You'll do no such thing!"

"Make up your mind." The playful twinkle in his blue eyes reassured her. "There's just no pleasing you some days, counselor. Pleasing you at night, luckily, is another story." Cupping her chin in his hand, he reminded her, "I want my dance tonight, no matter what happens with Caroline. Do we have a deal?"

"Definitely." She kissed his lips gently. "I guess we'd better bring the jewels with us for safekeeping. It's a factor in their favor, right, that they only pawned two of them in fifty years?"

"Two that we know of, you mean."

Josie sent him a withering glare. "Right. Who knows how many they dismantled and sold on the international black market? That would explain the castle in Ireland and all Grandma's furs." Without waiting for him to reply, she instructed, "Just get the jewels and stop manufacturing arguments to use against her, or the dance is off."

He was chuckling as he ambled off toward the archway, and Josie decided to adopt his confident attitude despite the turmoil in her mind and heart at the thought of interrogating her sweet, frail, larcenous grandmother.

TWELVE

Caroline was waiting for them in a chair by the window, her binoculars resting in her lap and a brilliant smile shining on her face. It broke Josie's heart to know that the sweet little criminal had seen them carrying the jewels up from the beach and now actually believed she'd gotten away with this ridiculous scheme.

"Is that them?" Caroline demanded, eyeing the burlap bundle under Locke's arm with unrestrained delight. "Can I see them? This is so exciting! I'm so proud of you two for finding them." She raised her gaze to Locke's and added solemnly, "I'm sure your grandfather is very proud of you too."

"Don't say any more to Locke, Grandma. He's going to go put the jewels in the hotel safe while you and I have a little chat."

Caroline's expression grew wary. "Couldn't I just see them first? Everyone says they were just beautiful."

"Cut it out, Grandma." Josie was surprised by the hurt she heard in her own voice and took a deep breath before explaining more gently, "I don't want you to talk in front of Locke yet. He wants to help us, and of course we trust him, but it's my job . . ."

The flood of tears in the older woman's eyes—eyes that easily rivaled the most beautiful emeralds in the Greybill collection—made Josie fall to her knees and embrace her mournfully. "I'm so sorry, sweetie. Please don't be frightened. Nothing bad is going to come from this, I promise you. Just tell me the truth—the whole truth—and then I promise I'll take care of the rest."

"Josie's right," Locke added softly. "I know this is painful for you, but just get it over with so we can help you put it behind you."

"I'm so ashamed." Caroline was sobbing so deeply, they could barely make out her words. "I wanted to tell you. Both of you. It's not that I didn't trust you. I was just so embarrassed—"

"Wait." Josie turned pleading eyes to Locke. "Could you just step out onto the deck for a minute?"

"No, Josie. I want Locke to hear everything. He deserves that after all the trouble I've caused him."

Locke knelt beside the pair and insisted huskily, "You haven't caused me trouble, Caroline. You've brought me more fun and happiness than you know. You brought me and Josie together, didn't you? You can see for yourself what a great match that was. A little inconvenience and a few white lies are a small price to pay for that."

"Look at you." Caroline touched his face in wonder. "You have the same expression your grandfather had fifty years ago. So filled with gentleness and compassion."

"And love," Locke added quietly. "You see that too, don't you?"

"I want you to stay and listen to the story, please?"

"That's up to your lawyer."

They both turned to Josie, who had to smile at the earnest need in their eyes. "He's gorgeous and I love him, Grandma, but he's also a cop, so he's out of here. Okay?"

Caroline dabbed at her eyes, then assumed a matriarchal air. "I have the right to remain silent and to talk to an attorney, but I also have the right to waive those rights. Don't I, Locke?"

He grinned uncomfortably. "Ask Josie."

Caroline frowned. "I have the right to fire her and represent myself, don't I?"

"You can fire a lawyer, but you can't fire a granddaughter."

Josie sent him a grateful glance. "You're putting Locke in a bad position, Grandma. If he hears anything incriminating, it's his duty to report it to his superiors."

"Incriminating?" Caroline bit her lip. "He already knows that your grandfather and I killed Mr. Greybill and stole the jewels. What else could I say that would be worse than that?"

Josie sank onto the floor and nodded. "Nice work, Grandma. Locke, I guess you can stay now. Feel free to give her legal advice too, because I'm not going to bother trying anymore."

"Don't sulk," Caroline scolded. "It's not becom-

ing. Go get us a pitcher of lemonade and some
glasses, and then I'll tell you both the whole story."

Darkness was settling on Driftwood Point and the
band was beginning to play its familiar set of dance
tunes when Caroline Galloway began to tell her story.
"I had known your grandfather since the day I was
born, which was twenty-three years before we got
married. We almost didn't take a honeymoon at all.
Money was tight, and we knew each other so well, it
didn't seem necessary. But he insisted on bringing
me here, so that we could spend time alone together,
the way you can never do in a small town. And from
the moment we got here, he was very romantic and
attentive, calling me his bride and showering me with
attention and telling me all the plans he had for our
future. He wanted to take care of me and spoil me."

Caroline paused to focus on Josie. "That's probably
the most important thing you need to understand
from all this. You're so independent and feisty. I was
nothing like you. It's strange, because the resem-
blance between us is so strong otherwise."

"You're stronger than you think you are,
Grandma," Josie assured her. "Look what you've accomplished in your life. Raising a wonderful son,
then single-handedly rescuing his babies and raising
them when he died so young. You put me and the
boys through school—"

"I had to learn to be tough," Caroline agreed. "But
it wasn't in my nature. My nature was to be shy and

delicate and easily flustered. That's the girl who came here fifty years ago.

"I was pretty too, just like you are now. I didn't have many fancy clothes, but I had one glamorous dress, and I wore it for your grandfather the night of the party at the big house. I wanted to be the most beautiful, desirable girl there."

"I'll bet you were too," Locke interrupted.

"Unfortunately," Caroline sighed, "I attracted the wrong kind of attention."

Josie tried unsuccessfully to read between those lines. "What does that mean?"

"Your grandfather and I were dancing. I was a little dizzy, and so he left me leaning against a trellis while he went to find something cool for me to drink. But I was afraid I might lose my dinner right there in front of all those society folks, and so I moved farther into the shadows, away from the crowd."

"Onto the veranda?"

Caroline nodded. "I didn't realize that our host, Mr. Greybill, was right in the next room until he came out and spoke to me, scaring me half to death. I thought that I must have looked awful—pale and nauseous and all that. But he was very solicitous and invited me into his study for some brandy. I told him I'd rather just wait for your grandfather, but he offered to have someone go and fetch him, and I simply didn't see the harm." She smiled sadly. "You would have realized what he was up to, I'm sure. But I was so naive."

"He was hitting on you?" Josie patted her grandmother's hand. "He sounds like a real jerk. I take it he didn't send for Grandpa?"

"He settled me onto a sofa and gave me some brandy. I sipped it, just a little. The fumes were strong, and they really helped clear my head a little. I was grateful. I suppose he misinterpreted that—"

"Don't do that," Josie interrupted sharply. "He didn't 'misinterpret' anything. He took advantage of your innocent nature, just like you said. But you didn't do anything wrong."

"You make it sound as though . . . well, as though he forced himself on me, but it didn't start out that way. He was trying to seduce me. To charm me. That's why he opened the safe, you see? He wanted me to accept a ruby ring, in exchange for . . . well . . ."

"I hate this guy," Locke growled.

"I insisted that I needed to get back to the party, and then he grew a little surly. That was when I first realized he'd probably had too much to drink. I tried to leave, but he pushed me back down, and then suddenly your grandfather was there. He grabbed Greybill and punched him, right in the face, and sent him flying into a piece of furniture. You could hear his head crack against a sharp edge, and you just knew without a doubt that he was dead."

"Thank heavens Grandpa got there in time," Josie breathed. "He was a hero, Grandma. Why didn't you tell Locke's grandfather what really happened?"

Caroline smiled sadly. "If we had realized what a gentleman the investigator would be, we might have considered that. But we panicked. Greybill and his guests were powerful people, Josie. I was terrified that they'd send your grandfather to prison, just when . . . just when . . ."

"Just when you'd realized how much you loved him?"

Caroline nodded. "He decided we should make it look like a robbery, and so he took the jewels, and bundled them up, and hid them in a compartment in the trunk of our car. He'd had one custom built for transporting payroll and other important papers for the shop. And by some miracle the officers who searched all the vehicles didn't find it."

"And so you told them you'd been on the veranda the whole time?"

"Exactly. Fortunately, there were witnesses who had seen me on the dance floor. They said my face was white as a ghost. And the waiters remembered your grandfather pestering them for ice and a rag for my forehead, so we weren't really treated as suspects, although in a sense, everyone was. I was the star witness, and they badgered me constantly. Your poor grandfather was beside himself trying to make them leave me alone." Turning to Locke, she confided, "It was only when the FBI arrived that I was treated courteously. I know I should have trusted them, but by then I was so very frightened, I just wanted to go home."

"That's understandable, Caroline."

"We were going to return the jewels when the time was right. But the time was never right. Once Josie's father was born, I was terrified that the authorities might not believe us and might send my husband to prison. I didn't want my son to grow up without a father. And then so much time passed, and there always seemed to be a reason to wait. Then, of course, when I was so unexpectedly made a widow, I simply didn't know what to do. I wanted to mail them anonymously to the FBI, but I wasn't quite sure how to do it. So I decided to hide them away and make a full confession in my will.''

"Then I showed up?"

"No," Josie interrupted. "Before you showed up, Grandma pawned two pieces of jewelry." Turning to Caroline, she added quickly, "It's okay, sweetie. I know you needed the money to help Johnny with school. It was darling of you to take that risk for us."

"I had put you and Ted through school." Caroline nodded. "It didn't seem fair to tell him that I couldn't help him when his turn came."

"He would have understood. And I would have started paying you back. I'm going to do that starting now—"

"Nonsense, Josie. It was my pleasure to give you the gift of education. And it's not as though I'm poverty stricken. I simply didn't want to liquidate any assets at that particular time."

"You're such a liar," Josie sighed. "I love you, but you're really pathological. Just admit that you don't have any money—"

"That's enough." Caroline's eyes reprimanded her as sharply as her tone. "I'm certainly not going to discuss my finances with you, young lady. And just for the record, I fully intended to redeem the jewels before anyone was the wiser. I just didn't anticipate they'd be recognized."

Locke was grinning fondly. "Okay, so now we're back to the best part of the story. I showed up. Right?"

"Yes." Caroline beamed. "I knew from the moment you appeared on my doorstep that you were going to solve two problems at one time for me."

"The jewels *and* the spinster granddaughter?"

"Exactly. I was so certain I could hide the jewels and allow you to find them. But I had forgotten how steep those awful steps are. That's why it was such a perfect opportunity when you decided to go to Los Angeles. I could take my time on the steps without being afraid you'd see what I was doing." She grimaced at the memory. "I made it down them with no problems, although it took quite a while. Then I managed to place the jewels in the rocks, although that wasn't as easy as it sounds. I was so exhausted that I lost my footing on the way back up."

"I'm so sorry, Grandma."

"It would have been much worse if I'd fallen on the way down," Caroline soothed. "They would have found me in a heap with incriminating evidence right in my hands, and you two hundreds of miles away and unable to advise me! In that sense it all went quite well, don't you think?"

"Smooth as silk," Josie drawled.

Caroline moistened her lips before she spoke again. "I think we'll have to make a deal, Josie. I can't possibly bear the embarrassment of a trial—"

"Trial?" Locke scoffed. "The only person who should have been tried was Greybill, and he's dead.

There won't be any charges, Caroline. I can guarantee you that."

Her eyes brimmed instantly with tears of relief. "Are you sure they'll believe me?"

"I'll see to it. In fact, I can almost guarantee you it'll be taken care of quietly if the Greybill family has anything to say about it. There are buildings and hospital wings named after that jerk, and I'm sure they don't want the world to find out he was an attempted rapist."

"I never said that," Caroline scolded. "He was persistent, but—"

"Just let me and Locke handle it," Josie interjected firmly. "Please?"

"I suppose. As long as you promise to tell them how sorry I am. And tell them I promise to pay back every cent I got from pawning the jewels."

"According to Bureau records, you only got three thousand dollars, right? We can deduct that from the fifty-thousand-dollar reward," Locke smiled. "That still leaves forty-seven thousand for you."

Josie's pulse quickened. "You think they'll still give her the reward?"

"If they don't, they may be reading some very unpleasant things about their patriarch in the morning paper."

"That's enough," Caroline protested. "I won't be part of any blackmail scheme, young man."

Josie almost laughed out loud at the chagrined expression on Locke's face. "Homicide and robbery are okay, but blackmail's out. Is that how it goes, Grandma?"

"It isn't blackmail," Locke grumbled. "It's just common sense. Look at all the trauma she's experienced because of Greybill's assault. They'll be glad that this goes away without a lawsuit and ugly publicity."

"Fifty thousand dollars," Caroline murmured. "Do you realize what you can do with that? Josie, you could put a down payment on a house! And, Locke, if you don't already have investments, this is the perfect way to start. Twenty-five thousand dollars apiece is a wonderful nest egg—"

"I can't take the reward." Locke chuckled. "Finding the jewels was my *job*, Caroline."

"Well, Josie can make a gift of half of it to you," Caroline sniffed. "If your boss has a problem with that, he can come and talk to me, and I'll tell him how lucky he is—"

"Grandma!"

Startled, Caroline turned to her granddaughter and explained, "I thought you'd *want* to share it. After all, we couldn't have done this without him."

Josie turned to Locke. "We should have known when she ordered those clams that she'd really gone 'round the bend."

"I beg your pardon?" Caroline frowned.

"I think what Josie's trying to say is, we want you to have the money. *All* of the money."

"Don't be silly! What do I need forty-seven thousand dollars for? You two are just starting out. I know you both have good jobs, and I couldn't be prouder, but life has a way of catching you by surprise." She smiled wistfully. "I never dreamed I'd be widowed and raising three darling grandchildren, but it happened. You need to be better prepared than I was."

Before Josie could offer sympathy, Caroline continued. "The most important thing is to buy yourselves some real estate and pay it off as soon as possible. Then you'll always have homes, at the very least."

"But we want that for *you,*" Josie protested. "We want you to use the reward money to save your house. Doesn't that make more sense?"

Caroline stared at Josie as though she were from outer space. "What an odd idea. What do I need a house for?"

"Pardon?"

"Your brothers have been begging me to come and live with them. Johnny even offered to add on a little apartment, just for me, at his place."

"And that appeals to you?"

"To watch his little darlings for him? Absolutely. But I had my responsibilities to you to think of."

"*Par*don?" Josie didn't know whether to laugh or scream. After all her fine talk of not needing a man to take care of her, was Caroline actually implying that she'd needed her grandma to fill that role?

The irony hadn't been lost on Locke, who suggested impishly, "Now that Josie has me in her life, you can go to San Diego without worrying about her anymore."

Caroline nodded. "That makes sense, except you two live so far apart from one another. That's why I think she needs to use the reward money to invest in a home of her own. I know you'll do your best, Locke, but she's a difficult girl, and I can't leave until I'm sure she'll be all right."

Before Josie could shriek in frustration, Locke grabbed her hand and pulled her to her feet.

"Excuse us, Caroline. I need to borrow your granddaughter for a minute or two."

"Locke?" Jose protested. "What are you doing?

"You promised me this dance," he reminded her firmly.

Caroline smiled impishly. "Go ahead. The fireworks will be starting any minute."

Despite her better judgment, Josie simply had to go with him onto the deck. Still, she couldn't help but demand as soon as they were out of Caroline's earshot, "Have you lost your mind?"

"If I have, I'm in good company," he said, chuckling. "Come here." He rested his hands on her hips and urged her to sway to the music. "Our dance, remember?"

"Interesting timing." Josie smiled as she succumbed to the temptation to move against him.

"I've decided to adopt the Galloway method of dealing with problems."

"Oh?"

He nodded confidently. "We pretended to come up here for romance when we were really coming to get the reward, and it worked out pretty well. Right?"

Josie nodded, fascinated by the amorous gleam in his eye.

"So, I'm willing to try another charade. For Caroline's sake."

"A charade?"

He dropped the bantering tone. "You went to law school at UCLA. But you went back to Sutterville after graduation, even though all your connections were in Southern California, because you didn't want Caroline to be alone. Right?"

"What's your point?"

"You've been staying in Sutterville to take care of Caroline, and she's been staying there to take care of you. It's crazy."

"I agree." Josie rested her cheek against Locke's chest and sighed. "She should move to San Diego and live with Johnny immediately."

"And you'll buy a house in Sutterville?" he scoffed. "Are you that attached to the place?"

Josie shrugged. "Attached? Not really, but I have a practice there now."

"A practice that barely supports you. Because there just aren't enough criminals there. You need to move to a crime-ridden big city."

Josie smiled at the thought. She *could* move to San Diego, couldn't she? She'd love being near her brothers, not to mention her mom and stepdad. And Grandma, of course. And she'd be so close to L.A., she and Locke could see each other every weekend. If that's what he was thinking, it was not only a good idea, it was a sweet compliment, especially from a confirmed bachelor.

"San Diego's beautiful—"

"San Diego?" he scoffed. "I'm talking about Los Angeles. We can fix you up with all the criminals you need. But to make this plan work . . ." He lowered his voice as though they were plotting a high-level conspiracy. "We have to convince Caroline that you're going to live happily ever after. With a husband and a mortgage and all the trimmings."

"Husband?" Josie pulled free and stared intently into his deep blue eyes.

"It's the only way to convince her to move," he explained cheerfully. "We'll pretend to be madly in love with each other. You'll move in with me, and after a few months we'll pretend to get engaged. Then we'll have a wedding ceremony, a honeymoon—the whole works. That should fool her, don't you think?"

"Locke—"

"Hear me out, Josie. This plan is foolproof. We'll even use some of the reward money to get a nice place where she can come visit us whenever she wants. She'll get a big kick out of knowing she helped us buy our first place. And"—his voice became so low, it was positively seductive—"if she starts to get suspicious after a couple of years, we'll have a kid or two. Just to throw her off guard."

Josie gulped and admitted, "It's so crazy, it just might work."

For one brief second the twinkle in his eyes became a blaze of passion that warmed Josie to the core. Then he was grinning his maddening grin again. "You'll have to give the performance of a lifetime, you know, if we want to pull this off. For example . . ." His hands encircled her waist and he pulled her close again. "You have to kiss me like you can't live without me."

"And you'll pretend you can't live without me either?"

"Anything for Grandma." In apparent illustration of his commitment, he lowered his mouth to hers, kissing her as though life itself depended upon it. At that very moment the first booming volley of Driftwood Point fireworks shot through the darkness above the beach, splitting the quiet night with a shocking display of brilliant red, white, and blue lights.

Reeling, Josie slipped her hands behind his neck to steady herself before admitting breathlessly, "You're pretty convincing, Agent Harper. I'm beginning to think this plan isn't so crazy after all."

"She'll never suspect a thing," he assured her. "Of course, you have to break your anti-cop vow, but that's a small price to pay for Caroline's happiness. Right?"

"A very small price."

"So? You'll marry me?"

Josie smiled shyly and echoed his "Anything for Grandma," then pulled his head back down for a scintillating kiss that left no lingering doubts that their plan would be a complete success.

BOOK YOUR PLACE ON OUR WEBSITE
AND MAKE THE
READING CONNECTION!

We've created a customized website just for our very special readers, where you can get the inside scoop on everything that's going on with Zebra, Pinnacle and Kensington books.

When you come online, you'll have the exciting opportunity to:

- View covers of upcoming books
- Read sample chapters
- Learn about our future publishing schedule (listed by publication month *and author*)
- Find out when your favorite authors will be visiting a city near you
- Search for and order backlist books from our online catalog
- Check out author bios and background information
- Send e-mail to your favorite authors
- Meet the Kensington staff online
- Join us in weekly chats with authors, readers and other guests
- Get writing guidelines
- AND MUCH MORE!

Visit our website at
http://www.zebrabooks.com

COMING IN AUGUST FROM
ZEBRA BOUQUET ROMANCES

#57 BACHELORS INC: MARRYING OWEN
by Colleen Faulkner

____(0-8217-6667-8, $3.99) On the verge of beginning a new life in a new state, Abby Maconnal is finally ready to put her shattered marriage with Owen Thomas behind her. Just a quick stop at her ex's to pick up her things, and she'll be on her way—or so she thinks. A hurricane is about to strand Abby under Owen's roof . . . in Owen's arms!

#58 THE MEN OF SUGAR MOUNTAIN: THREE WISHES
by Vivian Leiber

____(0-8217-6668-6, $3.99) Dashing Winfield Skylar is back home and busy showing Zoe Kinnear how to take some risks. But the biggest challenge of all comes when she reveals the startling truth about the little boy with Skylar blood. Can Win finally let go of the past—and allow this woman and child to become his future?

#59 ASK ME AGAIN by Wendy Morgan

____(0-8217-6669-4, $3.99) Being a bridesmaid in a stuffy wedding isn't Patience Magee's idea of a good time. And now, she has to walk down the aisle with logical, unflappable Jace Hoffman as her escort. There's only one question haunting her—when did Jace turn into such a hottie, and how can she keep from falling for her total opposite?

#60 SILVER LINING by Susan Hardy

____(0-8217-6670-8, $3.99) Wealthy heiress Katherine Spencer doesn't remember anything—not the tornado, the blow to her head, or even her own name. All she knows is that from the moment farmer Tom Weaver took her in, she's felt strangely at home. And when Tom wraps her in his strong arms, she starts to believe that this is just where she belongs.

Call toll free **1-888-345-BOOK** to order by phone or use this coupon to order by mail.

Name _____

Address _____

City _____ State _____ Zip _____

Please send me the books I have checked above.

I am enclosing	$_____
Plus postage and handling*	$_____
Sales tax (in NY and TN)	$_____
Total amount enclosed	$_____

*Add $2.50 for the first book and $.50 for each additional book.

Send check or money order (no cash or CODs) to:

Kensington Publishing Corp. Dept. C.O., 850 Third Avenue, New York, NY 10022

Prices and numbers subject to change without notice. Valid only in the U.S.

All books will be available 8/1/00. All orders subject to availability.

Visit our website at **www.kensingtonbooks.com**.